REUNION

A NOVEL BY

Allyson Braithwaite Condie

DESERET
BOOK
SALT LAKE CITY, UTAH

For the friends of my life

All rights reserved. No part of this book may be reproduced in any form or by any means without permission in writing from the publisher, Deseret Book Company, P. O. Box 30178, Salt Lake City, Utah 84130. This work is not an official publication of The Church of Jesus Christ of Latter-day Saints. The views expressed herein are the responsibility of the author and do not necessarily represent the position of the Church or of Deseret Book Company.

This book is a work of fiction. The characters, places, and incidents in it are the product of the author's imagination or are represented fictitiously.

DESERET BOOK is a registered trademark of Deseret Book Company.

Visit us at DeseretBook.com

Library of Congress Cataloging-in-Publication Data

Condie, Allyson Braithwaite.

(CIP on file)

ISBN 978–1–59038–989–8

Printed in the United States of America
Publishers Printing, Salt Lake City, UT

10   9   8   7   6   5   4   3   2   1

CONTENTS

CONTENTS

CAST OF CHARACTERS

***The three main narrators for* Reunion:**

Addie Sherman: Addie loves snowboarding and hanging out with her group of guy friends. She appeared briefly in *Yearbook* and is the younger sister of Dave Sherman.

Sam Choi: Sam is part of Addie's group of friends. He is a younger brother of Michaela Choi from *Yearbook*.

Caterina (Cate) Giovanni: One of the main characters from *First Day*. Cate is now attending school at BYU–Idaho, a long way from her hometown of Ithaca, New York.

***Characters in* Reunion *whom you might remember from* Yearbook *and/or* First Day:**

Dave Sherman: Dave is Addie's older brother and the class clown from *Yearbook*. He married Avery Matthews in *First Day*.

Avery Matthews Sherman: She's the poetry-writing member of the newspaper staff in *Yearbook* who converted to the Church and married Dave Sherman in *First Day*.

Michaela (Mikey) Choi: Sam's older sister appeared in *Yearbook*, where she was instrumental in the conversion of Julie Reid. She also appeared briefly in *First Day*.

Ethan Beckett: Ethan dated Michaela Choi in *Yearbook* and served a mission to Brazil in *First Day*. He is Andrea Beckett's younger brother.

Andrea Beckett Hammond: The Homecoming Queen in *Yearbook* and the seminary teacher/Cornell student in *First Day*. Married Joel Hammond in *First Day*.

Joel Hammond: One of the main characters from *First Day*. Joel is a graduate student at Cornell University.

Steve Ward: One of Cate's best friends (and co-president of their seminary class in high school). He first appears in *First Day*.

Julie Reid: Julie is serving a mission in Scotland. Julie was converted to the church in *Yearbook*.

Mr. Thomas: An English teacher who retired at the end of *Yearbook*.

Tyler Cruz: The basketball player from *Yearbook* who befriended Julie. Tyler played college basketball for the University of Utah and makes a cameo appearance at the beginning of *First Day*.

DECEMBER

He called the Seattle Washington Temple early to make sure he could have the exact date he wanted for the sealing. He liked the idea of choosing the day in June that had always been special to them.

As he had hoped, there was no problem scheduling this far in advance. He put down the phone and looked out the window at the gray rain of a Pacific Northwest December. It might well be raining again in June, but then the landscape would be alive, with flowers everywhere, and less of a chill in the air. It would be beautiful. Six months to go.

He wondered if he would be ready. He wondered if she would be ready.

DECEMBER

Addie Sherman

The last few minutes of school each day are always the worst, but they're even longer on Fridays. The weekend is so close you can taste it.

I stole another look at my watch. Only a few seconds until the final bell. I eased my book closed and put the lid on my pen. I didn't want to lose any time on my way out the door, so I started inching my legs out into the aisle. That way, I could be the first one to stand up and bolt.

"Addie Sherman, I see you," Mr. Hughes called from the front of the classroom. "Take your assignment back out. Class isn't over yet—you should still be working."

His timing was terrible. Right as he finished speaking, the bell rang, and I shot to my feet and headed for the door. "Next time, I'm going to make you stay after!" he called, but I kept on going.

I smiled to myself as I ran down the hall. I navigated the crowded areas as though I were in a slalom race, turning and shifting my balance, and gliding around every object in my path without losing any speed. I was headed for the finish line—the parking lot. The minute I left school grounds, Friday would *really* begin.

Friday. The best day of the week. The day I always went snow-boarding with my friends after school. My gear was already packed and waiting for me in my car. My snowboard was waxed and the edges were sharpened. And, according to the weather reports on the radio, there was supposed to be at least four inches of fresh snow on the mountain.

On the way to my locker, I saw Rob Patrick and Sam Choi, two of the guys I always go boarding with. They were heading in the other direction, toward the parking lot where we meet to carpool.

"You comin'?" Rob called to me, and I yelled back, "Yeah, I'll meet you out there." He nodded and the crowd swallowed them up again.

A bright red piece of paper fluttered from every locker in the hall, mine included. I ripped it off, looked at it, and grimaced in disgust. It was a flier reminding us that the Holiday Formal, one of the biggest dances of the winter, was only two weeks away. I had seen posters advertising the dance all over the halls of the school. I didn't need my very own copy stuck to my very own locker, thank you very much. I didn't need to be reminded that I wasn't going. That I had, as a matter of fact, never been to a guys' choice dance, even though I'd been sixteen for ten months.

I refused to let it dampen my mood. It was Friday, and I was out of there. I grabbed the books I needed for the weekend and slammed my locker shut. On my way out the door, I dunked my flyer into the closest trash can and started running.

I reached my car at the same time the guys pulled up next to it.

"You're holding us up, Sherman!" Rob called out the window, grinning.

"Calm down," I said, as though I hadn't been in a hurry myself. I hooked my board onto the rack of Rob's car and climbed into the front seat next to him. It was my turn to ride shotgun.

"Hey," I said to Cody and Sam in the backseat.

"*Four* inches of snow this morning," Cody said in response, gesturing at the radio. We all grinned. Rob turned up the volume and we were gone.

We were escaping, the way we did every Friday. No going to boring basketball games to cheer for other people instead of doing something ourselves. No standing around at stupid post-game dances. No sitting in each other's living rooms trying to decide what to do. During snowboarding season, we knew exactly where we'd be and what we'd be doing every single Friday night. We'd be up at Snoqualmie Pass, snowboarding until they turned the lights out. Then we'd drive home, worn-out and completely happy.

• • •

It usually took about an hour to get to the Pass from the suburb of Seattle where we lived. We all rode together so we could split the cost of the gas with Rob, who always drove because his car was the most reliable. Not that that was saying much. Sam and Cody didn't have access to cars on a regular basis, and mine was so old and wretched that my snowboard was worth more than it was. My older brothers had each trashed the car in different ways, and my dad kept resurrecting it to live another day. Lucky me.

"Gas money," Rob reminded us. We all stuck some wadded-up bills into the cupholder at the front of the car.

"Is it cool if I pay in pennies?" Cody asked. He was teasing. I think. You never knew with Cody.

"Sure," Rob said sarcastically. "You can count it out while you're riding in the trunk."

I laughed and looked over at Rob. Rob Patrick is impossibly good-looking any day of the week, but put him in a hat and jacket and set him on a snowy slope on a gorgeous Friday afternoon, and it's hard not to develop a crush on him. I think it's the combination of dark eyes and dark hair with an absolutely flat-out radiant smile.

I pulled a box of cheap, gas-station donuts out of my backpack and offered one to Rob. He took a couple. Before I could even offer them to Cody and Sam, Cody reached up and grabbed the box.

"Mmmm," he said. "You're the best, Addie."

I rolled my eyes. "Help yourself, Cody."

"You can have some of my jerky," Cody said, handing me a stick.

"Disgusting," I told him, like I always do, but then I took some anyway and ate it, like I always do.

Sam laughed at me. "Hypocrite."

I shrugged and laughed too.

I'm used to snowboarding with guys. It all began when I was eleven and my mom made my brothers take me along when they went. I took to it right away, mainly because my brothers showed no mercy. One of my older brothers, Dave, gave me his old board. They helped me go down the bunny run a couple of times, and then they left me to it. I learned the rest from watching them and following them around the slopes. Dave always kept an eye on me, but mostly I took care of myself.

I loved snowboarding from that first run down the hill. I knew it was what I wanted to do, and nothing could stop me, even though I fell a lot. I tagged along every single time my brothers went, and I was always the last one to want to leave the mountain. Even my parents recognized that my obsession was not going to go away. My mom made a deal with me. If I kept taking dance until I was twelve, she would buy me any board I wanted, and I could quit dancing and focus on snowboarding. We both kept our end of the bargain. The day I turned twelve, I went to my last dance class, and then she drove me straight to the sporting goods store.

• • •

We were nearing the resort, so I tucked the last couple of donuts away in my bag and pulled out two elastic bands. I braided my hair in two braids. As I turned my head to the side to finish the right braid, I caught Rob looking over at me thoughtfully. He opened his mouth to speak, but he was interrupted before he said a word.

"Do you think *my* hair's long enough to braid yet?" Sam asked, sticking his head between our seats.

"Not even close," I told him, laughing. "It's barely long enough to cover the tops of your ears." Sam had been growing his hair out since last year when we teased him too much about his "Marine haircut." It hadn't been short at all, but apparently he'd decided to grow it longer like Rob and Cody.

"We could cut off one of Ad's braids and clip it to your hair at the back," Rob suggested.

"Like a Jedi," I offered, and Sam started laughing, falling back in his seat.

Rob was looking ahead at the road again, instead of at me. I reached into my bag a final time, fishing out a beanie and pulling it onto my head. The beanie was an old brown-and-orange one of my brother's and was unbelievably ugly. "What do you think?" I asked the guys, turning my head to model it for them.

"You look like a tiger," commented Cody through a mouthful of beef jerky. "Do you think it will turn out to be *the one?*"

"We'll see." I wore a different hat almost every time we went snowboarding. I was trying to find my good-luck hat. All three of the guys had good-luck hats that they wore only when they really needed them, like when they were in a competition or something like that. I'd tried old ones, new ones, borrowed ones . . . but I hadn't found the right one yet.

"It looks cool," Rob told me. "Kinda old-school."

"It used to be my brother's."

"Which one? Dave?" Sam asked.

"How'd you guess?" I joked. Sam Choi is a year older than I am, and he and I are in the same stake. Our older siblings are friends, and we've known each other for years. We all know the other Mormons in our area pretty well because there aren't that many of us. Sam was the reason I was part of this whole snowboarding group in the first place. Early last winter, we'd gone boarding for a combined stake Young Men/Young Women activity. Sam and I were the only ones who had any experience, so we hung out a lot that trip. Afterward, he'd invited me to come with him and his friends every Friday, where I'd gotten to know Rob. Cody, I'd known since elementary school.

The timing had been perfect. My brothers had all moved out by then and my best friend, Cheryl, had moved to Boston, so I was lonely.

People tell me all the time that I'm quiet, and I've heard myself described as shy. I don't think I'm shy. I just take my time warming up to people, unlike my brothers, who try (and often succeed) to make everyone into their instant best friend. Making friends doesn't come as easily to me.

But, if I truly *were* shy, you'd think being the only girl in the group of three cute guys would make me even more so. I *was* pretty quiet the first few times we went. I wanted them to know I was serious about boarding and wasn't coming along to try to flirt with them, so I hardly said anything. As the weeks passed, it got easier and easier to talk to them. And now, I can hold my own. Usually.

"Does anyone have more jerky?" Cody asked from the back.

"No, and I don't think you should have any more," I told him firmly. "The rest of us won't be able to ride back with you if you do."

"She's right, Cody," Rob said. "Sorry, dude."

"Man," said Cody, and he lapsed into silence.

The nice thing about hanging out with guys is I don't have to talk if I don't want to. I don't have to pretend to be someone I'm not. I'm Addie, I'm fun to be around, and I can hold my own with anyone on the slopes.

Cody belched loudly.

The bad thing is they honestly do see me as one of the guys. It's my blessing and my curse.

• • •

Still, I like boarding with the boys. There's no fussiness about things. If we want to board together, we do. If we want to take off on our own, we do that instead.

I carved my way down the mountain a few times by myself, getting the feel of the snow and enjoying the wind in my face. Partway down the fifth or sixth run, Rob flew in front of me and came to a stop in my path, cutting me off. I had to stop so fast I sprayed snow all over him.

"Careful, Ad," he said, wiping his face.

"What's the matter, were you scared?" I asked him, smiling. "You're the one who cut *me* off."

He laughed. "Yeah, but I cut it close. I started to think you weren't going to be able to stop, but you did. You're getting better than all of us, even Cody."

"I'm not as fast as Cody is."

"He's wild, though. You never know what's going to happen."

"That's for sure."

He gestured toward the little lodge at the bottom of the hill. "I've gotta run inside for a minute, but I need to talk to you. Can I catch back up with you when I get out?"

"Of course," I told him. What did he want to talk about? What was it that he kept trying to bring up? I couldn't help it. I felt hopeful. Was he going to ask me to the dance?

Rob smiled at me. "Awesome." Then he pointed ahead of him. "Go on. Let's see if I can catch you."

He couldn't. Especially not with my few seconds' head start, and not with the little charge of excitement that was running through my veins. I made it to the bottom way before he did.

Sam was standing by the lift, so I slid in next to him. "Hey," he said as we moved into the line together. "I've been trying to catch up with you all afternoon."

"What's up?" I looked back over my shoulder to see Rob disappear through the doors of the lodge.

"What are you grinning about?" he asked, following my gaze.

"Nothing." We got on the lift together, the chair bumping the backs of our legs in a familiar way. I was still smiling like an idiot, so to cover my tracks I said, "I just wasted Rob on that run."

Sam smiled. "Nice work." Then he paused. "Hey, you know the dance coming up?"

"Uh-huh," I said, and thought, *Here we go again.* Every time there was a formal dance at school, Sam and Cody asked my advice on who to take and what to do on the date. Rob, thankfully, had never made me go through the whole "help me ask her out" fiasco. I'd been especially thankful for that since I'd started liking him. Nothing pours salt in the wound like having to help the guy you like ask another girl out on a date. Even helping out guys who are just friends can get old.

"I'm not going to be able to go because my family's going out of town this year for the holidays," Sam said.

"That's too bad," I told him. "But you went to Homecoming. There are other dances. You'll be fine."

"Well, I know *that*," Sam said, as if I'd missed the point. But what the point was, I couldn't see. After a brief pause, he asked, "Are *you* going yet?"

Like an idiot, I smiled. I couldn't help myself. "No."

"Then why are you smiling? You *are* going with someone, aren't you?"

"I promise, I'm not."

The lift dropped us off, and Sam beat me down the run. I went more slowly than usual, making wider turns and watching the swoops my board cut into the snow. What would I say if Rob asked me to go to the dance with him? I'd say yes, of course. Then I'd have to find a dress to wear, since I couldn't wear one of my Sunday dresses to a formal dance. That would be a pain. But it would be worth it.

Rob still wasn't out of the lodge when I got to the bottom. I could see him through the big window, talking on his cell phone, and I wondered who he was calling. I turned back to the lift. This time it was Cody waiting for me.

"Adelaide," he said with a wide grin.

I frowned. He only calls me by my full name when he wants something. "Let's cut to the chase," I said. "What do you want to know—who to ask, or how to ask her?"

"What are you talking about?" Cody looked at me as if I were insane.

"Isn't that what you wanted to ask? It's what everyone else seems to want to know."

"Oh, that. No. I'm going with Cari. I asked her today."

"You did? Way to step up to the plate, Cody. I didn't even know you were thinking about asking her."

"I decided I was sick of making such a big deal out of it," Cody said. "I thought, I'll ask a girl who's cute and easy to hang out with, and I'll ask her the next time I see her instead of coming up with some whole big setup. It seemed to work. She said yes, which is the whole point anyway, right?"

"Right," I said. Would that be how Rob would ask me, if he did? I couldn't help but picture how things would be. The four of us on a date. Me with Rob, and Cari with Cody. I couldn't have picked a more fun group for my first date. Too bad Sam would be out of town.

If *Rob asks you,* I told myself. I turned to Cody. "So what *did* you want to ask me?"

"I wanted to ask if you wanted to go boarding tomorrow. I don't have to work this Saturday. Rob can't make it, but Sam's coming. I can drive."

"I want to, but I can't. Remember the deal I have with my parents?" I reminded him. I was allowed to go snowboarding every Friday as long as I kept my grades up and spent Saturday on homework.

Cody groaned. "Oh, right. Too bad. It's supposed to be great again tomorrow."

"Don't rub it in or anything," I told Cody, as Rob finally emerged from the lodge and waved to us.

"You going on another run right now?" Cody asked.

"Yeah, but I promised Rob I'd ride up with him." Although technically the lifts can fit three, we'd agreed long ago to only ride two at a time. We're friends, but smashing three of us on a chairlift in all our gear never ends well.

"Fine," said Cody, pretending to be offended. "See you in a minute." He made a face at Rob as he left.

"What was that all about?" Rob asked me.

"I told him I was riding up with you," I said, then felt embarrassed for some reason, like I'd said more than I should have. Rob didn't seem to notice.

"Let's go then."

Finally. *This* was the lift ride I'd been waiting for. Rob and I hopped on, and he turned to me immediately after we cleared the ground.

"I'm so glad I finally got you alone. I needed to talk to you without the other guys listening in. I have to ask you something."

"Oh?" I asked, my heart beating faster. "What is it?"

"Are you done with your essay for English yet? The one that's due on Monday?"

"No," I said, surprised and deflated. "I'm going to work on it tomorrow." Why did we have to be alone for him to ask me *that?*

Rob groaned. "That's too bad. I needed your help tomorrow."

"Oh?" My interest was piqued again.

"I'm going to ask Brook Stewart to the Holiday Formal, but I want to ask her in a cool way, you know, and I thought, maybe you might have some ideas for me." He said it all in one breath then looked at me, embarrassed. "I know I don't usually ask you about this stuff, but it's different this time. I want to do it right."

I was lucky that my face was windburned and red anyway. I would have flushed with humiliation right then. "I didn't know you liked Brook."

Brook Stewart was younger than we were, a sophomore, and she went to a different high school. We all knew her, however—Sam and I because she was in the same stake we were in, and Rob and Cody had met her at a few group activities they'd gone to with us. Of course Brook was cute and bubbly and blonde—all the things I'm not. Of course I should have known Rob wouldn't be thinking about taking me to the dance. Of course.

Rob looked embarrassed. "Well, she's cool. You know?"

"Is she even sixteen years old yet? Remember, Mormons usually can't date until then."

"I know. I checked. She turned sixteen a couple of weeks ago. I thought it would be fun to take her to her first dance, so that's why I want to ask her in a cool way."

You thought it would be fun to take her to her first dance, I repeated to myself silently. What about me? I was still waiting for *my* first dance, and it didn't look like the wait would be over any time soon.

Luckily, we were nearing the end of the lift ride. I didn't have to stall much longer. I'm a good friend, but not *that* good a friend. Not a good enough friend to tell Rob how to ask someone else to a dance I wanted to go to with him. Not this time.

"And you think I've got ideas for this?" I asked. Did he honestly have no idea that I'd never even been to a dance?

"I guess I was thinking you might have some clue for what I could do . . ." Rob trailed off as we got ready to get off the lift. "You've always had ideas for Cody and Sam. I thought you might have one for me too—"

"Write her a freaking poem or something, Rob," I interrupted, shoving off the lift, snapping my other boot back into the clip, and heading down the slope without looking back.

Partway down the slope, I ripped off my hat—obviously *not* my lucky one—and let it fly away on the cold wind, the same wind that was blowing my braids behind me and streaking the tears from my eyes.

DECEMBER

Sam Choi

Cheesiest. Christmas. Ever. At the end of the day, my brother Alex and I agreed on that 100%.

At least it wasn't the *worst* Christmas ever. That was the Christmas when I was eleven. (I don't even want to think about that Christmas. My parents have since redeemed themselves, but get real. Who gives an eleven-year-old kid snowpant bibs for Christmas? Who knew they even made them in that size?)

Anyway, I should backtrack to how we ended up spending Christmas in Utah, where we don't live, instead of in Seattle, where we do.

Back in October, my mom got all crazy and "homesick" for a white Christmas. She grew up in Salt Lake City, where apparently there's lots of fluffy, white, perfect snow, but all the rest of us (my dad included) grew up in Seattle, which means we seldom experience what she calls a "true white Christmas."

For some reason, missing out on that seemed to bug her more this year, and she decided she had to make up for this major void in our lives. "Wouldn't it be great if we rented a cabin or a condo in

Utah and met up with Michaela there for the holidays?" Michaela, who we call Mikey, is my older sister. She goes to school in Utah, at BYU.

"Why not?" my dad asked. "I wouldn't mind seeing a truly *white* Christmas."

Alex and I tried to point out that we were Seattle kids. *White Christmas* was only a song to us. We liked our Christmases *gray*. We didn't feel deprived. We'd just as soon stay in Seattle and hang out with our friends. Then . . .

"You could go snowboarding a lot," my mom pointed out. "And Utah snow is supposed to be some of the best on earth. They get all of that powder, you know."

Alex and I both agreed that a white Christmas wouldn't be so bad after all.

• • •

I thought Mikey might not go for it, because when she comes home to visit she's always all about how happy she is to be here, saying things like, "Oh, Mom, this food is so amazing! Oh, I'm so glad to be home!" On and on like that.

But she loved the idea. I could hear her screaming through the phone. Then she called again a few minutes later. I answered.

"Can I talk to Mom?" she asked.

"No."

"Sam," she said, sounding exasperated. "Come on. Put her on the phone."

I handed the phone to Mom.

"Hi, honey." Mom paused. "Oh, yes? He's checked with his parents? I don't see why not. Let me check with your dad to make sure. You're welcome."

She hung up the phone and turned to my dad. "Ethan's going to spend Christmas with us, too, if that's all right with you, honey."

"I suppose it is," my dad said. "I'd have assumed he'd want to go home. Isn't this his first Christmas back from his mission?"

"Apparently he's going to fly home the day after Christmas, so he'll be there with his family for most of the holidays."

"They must be getting serious," Dad said. He didn't seem totally thrilled about the idea. He likes my sister's boyfriend, Ethan—we all do—but Mikey is his only daughter, and Dad's a little overprotective. If she didn't get married until she turned forty, that would be fine with him.

Mom gave Dad a look that wasn't hard to read. It was a look that said, "I'll tell you the rest later."

. . .

Cabins and condos up in the Park City and Salt Lake ski areas turned out to be more expensive than my parents had planned. My mom ended up making reservations for a condo at a ski resort farther south, a couple of hours from Provo.

"How's the snow there?" I asked.

"We'll find out," Mom said cheerfully. "Besides, the point is for us all to be together."

Dad could see the look on my face. "Don't worry. It's hard to go wrong with Utah snow."

We arrived in Utah three days before Christmas, so the airport was packed with skiers and holiday travelers. It took forever to get our luggage, since Alex and I both had snowboards, and my parents both brought their old skis. I was secretly hoping they would decide not to use them. I was pretty confident no one else on the slopes had skis that ancient. And don't even get me started on their ski boots.

Eventually we got all our bags together, found our rental van, and were on our way to pick up Mikey and Ethan in Provo. It had snowed the night before, and it about killed me when we drove past all the signs pointing to Park City and the other areas that must have been filled with fresh powder. The mountains looked amazing—tall and sharp and blue and white. I groaned, but my parents were too smart to take the bait and ask me what was wrong. They knew I wanted to sucker them into staying in the Salt Lake area. We kept on driving south to Provo, leaving the big resorts behind, one by one.

As we drove near BYU to pick up Mikey and Ethan, Mom pointed out the MTC. "Look, Sam! That's where you might be in a few months!"

The MTC sat there, a bunch of big, orange brick buildings planted squarely behind a black iron fence. But it didn't look like the missionaries were on total lockdown. At least the gate was open. A group of bundled-up missionaries walked toward the Provo Temple, laughing and talking with each other. The closeness of the mountains and all that perfect snow didn't seem to be driving *them* crazy. Maybe they had been brainwashed or reprogrammed.

Mom acted like we were on a safari and had spotted some unusual wildlife. "Oh, Sam, look! There are some missionaries, right there!" She was so excited she grabbed Dad's arm, which made him swerve.

"Try not to hit them," I muttered. I haven't talked to my parents about how I feel about a mission. Everyone assumes I'm going, but no one has ever asked *me* if I am. If they had, I'd tell them that I'm not so sure about it.

It isn't that I don't believe in the Church. I think it's true. But I don't know if I'm cut out to walk around and *tell* other people what I believe. I also don't know if I'm cut out for all those rules and things you can and can't do.

Both my parents went on missions. They have albums and albums full of pictures. When I was younger, I used to like to look at those pictures of my parents on their missions in different countries. They looked so young, and the places seemed cool and far away, exotic. In a lot of the pictures, my mom or my dad is standing next to someone all dressed in white who was about to get baptized. The people looked at the camera or at each other with smiling faces, as if they were thrilled. Sometimes they had serious faces, as if they knew that this decision would change their lives.

Mikey's boyfriend, Ethan, is always talking about how amazing his mission was and how it was the best two years of his life. It's been six months since he got home, and he can't stop relating every freaking thing that happens to an experience from his mission. But most just-back-from-the-field missionaries are like that. You can't get away from them telling you all about it.

It kind of seems like missions make you boring.

. . .

You know what else makes you boring? Being in love. Mikey is usually fun—for an older sister—but she was completely useless over the holidays. All she wanted to do was be with Ethan—watch movies with Ethan, snuggle with Ethan, go skiing with Ethan. Ethan. Ethan. Ethan.

Alex and I still had plenty to do. Mom had been right. The snowboarding was decent after all. The powder was sweet, easily better than Seattle. I missed the guys and Addie. Boarding with Alex wasn't too bad, but he couldn't keep up with me the way my friends could, and I always had to wait for him at the bottom.

My parents came skiing a few times too, and thankfully, they didn't shame themselves (or me). They were both out of practice, but still had decent form. Their skis, though . . . now, those were another story. Man, those things were old. You'd think they'd have been recalled by now. Also, Mom wore a puffy, hot-pink parka left over from her college years. It hurt your eyes to look at at.

"Geez, is Mom still wearing that coat?" Mikey asked me one day when we were all out on the slopes together. "At least we won't have any trouble finding her!"

I opened my mouth to respond, but she was already skiing away, catching up with Ethan.

The one time I got to talk to Mikey was when Ethan went

somewhere on a drive with my parents. For some reason, Mikey didn't go along, and Mom put the three of us kids to work making Christmas cookies in the kitchen of the condo. Mom had bought all the ingredients and had even remembered to bring cookie cutters from home so the cookies would be like the ones we baked there.

Mikey made the dough, and Alex and I cut out the shapes. We started to act stupid, which was just like old times.

"Look," Alex said, showing Mikey a gingerbread boy and girl. "This is you and Ethan." He'd smushed their hands together so they were holding hands.

Mikey rolled her eyes and grinned at him.

"You're wrong, Alex," I told him. "They should look like this." I mashed their heads together. "Now they're kissing."

Alex started to laugh. "Oooh, Ethan, I love you so much," he said in his highest voice, which was pretty high, since Alex was still waiting for his voice to change completely.

"You guys are *so* mature," said Mikey.

"So are you getting married or what?" Alex asked.

"We'll see." Mikey was concentrating on arranging the cookies on the sheet. She turned away and put them into the oven, but I saw a smile on her face.

So it was true. "No *way*," I said. It seemed crazy that she was actually going to get married. Did Mom and Dad know? They'd guessed it was serious before we came on the trip, but did they know that a wedding was in the works?

Suddenly it all came together. "Is that why Ethan's on that drive with Mom and Dad? Is he asking for their permission or something?"

She started blushing like crazy.

I was right about that too! "Oh, man, Mikey."

"Does this mean we have to wear tuxes at the wedding?" Alex whined.

"How do you know Ethan's the right guy?" I shoved Alex so he would stop asking stupid questions. Who cared about tuxes? We had to make sure our sister was making the right choice.

"I just am," she said.

"Because he's such a great kisser?" Alex teased, and I shoved him again.

"You guys, stop," Mikey said, laughing. "We can talk about all this once I'm actually engaged."

"I think we should talk about it now," I said. "You need approval from your brothers too, you know. Have Ethan come talk to us next."

"No kidding," Alex agreed.

Mikey cut out another cookie. "Over my dead body."

"Dead body!" Alex exclaimed. He looked at me, and I gave up trying to have a serious conversation. We couldn't pass up a reference to a dead body.

The two of us advanced on Mikey, who started backing up. "What? What are you guys doing? *Oh, no . . .*"

"This is your own fault," I reminded her as we carried her, kicking and screaming and laughing, to the living room. "You can only blame yourself. You're the one who invented this game."

"I didn't know you guys would grow up to be so big," she said, still laughing.

"Dead body" was a game we used to play when we were kids. Back then she was bigger than we were and she would sit on us and tickle us until we promised to never bother her again—over our dead bodies.

We tried to set her down on the floor, but she had learned some evasive tactics from watching us all those years. She kicked at Alex and twisted away from me. She made a break for it, running out into the snow-filled front yard of the condo in her socks. Alex and I followed her and stopped on the front step.

"Should we lock her out?" I asked Alex, only to get hit right in the face with a snowball he'd thrown.

"Traitor," I said, but then a snowball Mikey had made hit him in the back.

It was every Choi for himself. Or herself.

. . .

"Get up! It's Christmas morning!" Mikey was bouncing on my bed. What was wrong with her? Was she still on a sugar high from all the cookies we'd eaten the day before?

"It's too early," I told her. I didn't even bother opening my eyes. "Even Alex hasn't gotten up this early in years. Go back to bed and come get me at eight or nine. Or ten. Ten would be great."

"If I make pancakes, will that change your mind?"

"No," I said, trying to kick her off the bed. It didn't work. She dodged me and scooted away. She wasn't going to leave me alone.

"Make it French toast and we have a deal," I mumbled.

"All right!" She moved over to the next bed, where Alex was still snoring away, and started to harass him.

I could hear my parents moving around downstairs, and the rumble of Ethan's voice. Why was it that all the adults in the family were awake, and all the so-called kids—me and Alex—were still asleep? What horrible parallel universe was this?

Mikey didn't have any success in waking up Alex, but she was sure the smell of French toast would eventually do the trick. She was right.

. . .

The packages under the tree were all fairly small. Mom had had a smart idea—she made all of us take pictures of the gifts we were giving each other and then wrap those up instead of the actual gift. That way, we didn't have to cart all our gifts from Seattle only to turn around and haul them right back. So for the most part, Mikey and Ethan were the only ones opening real gifts.

I opened one from Alex. It was a picture of a jumbo bag of Skittles. "Thanks, Alex," I told him. I held up the picture. "This looks a lot like the bag of Skittles you were eating on the plane."

Alex was unfazed. "I'll buy you another one when we get back. Couldn't leave them there all alone."

Mikey opened the University of Washington sweatshirt I'd gotten for her. "Thanks, Sam!" she said, pulling it on over her head.

"I figured you needed a reminder of which school is the best."

"Where are you going next year, anyway? Did you apply to BYU?"

"I did, but I haven't heard from them yet. I'm still waiting to hear back from a few other schools too."

I expected Mom to add, "Or he might not wait a semester, he might go straight on his mission," but she was uncharacteristically silent on the subject. She'd been sort of distracted the whole morning.

All through the gift giving she seemed like she was waiting for something else. She did get excited about the present Alex and I had gotten for her. We gave her a gift certificate for painting the living room, which she'd been nagging Dad to help her with forever. She hugged us both when she opened it. "What a thoughtful gift."

We didn't tell her it had been Dad's idea. He hates painting more than any other household job, including cleaning out the garage.

"No problem," Alex and I told her, feeling generous. Well, at least I was. Alex was flipping through his stack of photos, grinning at the thought of all the presents waiting for him back home.

"I think that was the last present." Dad looked under the tree. There weren't any little boxes or envelopes left.

"Um," said Ethan, looking over at Mikey. "I still have a gift to give you." He seemed nervous. My parents gave each other meaningful looks.

"Where is it?" Mikey looked around. She was starting to smile.

"It's outside." He took Mikey's hand. "We'll be right back," he said to the rest of us.

• • •

Mom couldn't contain herself. The door had barely shut behind them before she was running to the window to peek out. "They're heading off to that little group of trees," she reported. "I wonder if he's hidden the ring out there or if he's bringing it with him."

"He'd have to be an idiot to hide an engagement ring in the snow," I pointed out.

Mom didn't pay any attention to me. "I can't see them anymore. Oh, wait—"

Dad was laughing. "Get away from the window, honey. Give them their privacy."

"What's going on?" Alex asked. "Is Ethan really going to ask Mikey to marry him?"

"It looks like it." I was glad Ethan hadn't decided to bust out the engagement ring in front of everyone. This felt awkward enough. And what if she said no?

I knew she wasn't going to say no, but hey—anything could happen.

"Wait and see," Dad told Alex.

When they came back in, Mikey and Ethan were both grinning from ear to ear. They'd probably been kissing. I hoped they had brushed their teeth after all the French toast they had eaten.

"We're getting married!" Mikey held out her hand. She was wearing a ring. "Isn't it beautiful?"

She obviously expected me to comment on the ring. I couldn't tell much about it except that it was shiny. "Yeah, it looks great."

"Congratulations, you two!" Mom had tears in her eyes. Dad did too, I think. Alex pretended to throw up into his stocking, but got distracted halfway through by a piece of candy he'd left in there and ate it instead.

"Congratulations," I told Mikey, echoing my parents. I gave her a hug. "So when's the big day?"

"We're thinking the middle of February, maybe Presidents' Day weekend," Mikey said.

Mom's eyes widened. "That soon?"

"If that works for you. We don't need to have a fancy reception. We'd like to keep it simple."

"Well, all right, honey. We can make that happen." Mom's eyes got even brighter. "So, can you tell us about the proposal?"

"It was perfect!" Mikey glowed, and Ethan grinned proudly. "Ethan took me outside to that little patch of trees. You know, the one right over there?"

Mom acted like she hadn't been spying the whole time and glanced out the window where Mikey was pointing. "Oh, yes."

"He'd been out earlier and hung a bunch of prisms from the branches. I don't know if you remember, Mom, but Ethan gave me a prism for Christmas that first year we started dating."

"I remember that," Mom said, smiling at Ethan. "It was such a sweet gift."

I bet his mom or someone else suggested that, I thought. Ethan was a decent guy, but I doubted most guys thought of prisms right off the bat when they were getting gifts for girls.

"It was absolutely *beautiful* out there, because the sun was shining through the prisms. And then Ethan knelt down in the snow and said that he had another prism that was smaller and that he hoped I would like it. He was holding the box with the ring. And then he said some really sweet things"—she gave Ethan a secretive smile—"and asked me to marry him, and I said yes!"

Dad put his arm around Ethan's shoulders. "We'll be glad to have you as part of our family, Ethan."

Ethan and Mikey beamed at him. Mom was blinking back happy tears.

Like I said: Cheesiest. Christmas. Ever.

I caught Alex's eye, and we both started edging out of the room toward our bedroom, where our snowboarding gear was. No one seemed to notice. They were all busy talking about which temple, who would be in the reception line, all of that.

We made our escape. And when I was riding the lift up to the top of the mountain, I had a totally selfish thought. Mikey's wedding might distract my parents from all the questions about a mission and school, at least for awhile. She and Ethan had bought me some time.

It was the best Christmas gift I could have asked for.

CHAPTER 3

JANUARY

Caterina Giovanni

"You're not crying," my mom remarked.

I laughed. "I know."

My parents and I were standing in the Syracuse Airport to say good-bye. People moved around us or gathered in their own little clusters to say their farewells. The one tiny restaurant over to the side of the concourse was empty, except for one bored cashier. I thought it all looked very familiar.

Of course, that was because a few months ago, in August, we'd been in the same place doing the same thing. I think even the cashier might have been the same one, but I could be wrong. Anyway, last time, as my mom so kindly pointed out, I *had* cried. But not too much!

"So what's different this time?" my dad teased. "You're not going to miss us as much?"

"That must be it," I joked.

Before, it had been my first real, long-term good-bye to my parents. I was their youngest child. My brothers and sisters had all gone off to school, left on missions, and gotten married. Farewells and good-byes in my family were common.

I had always wondered which was harder: being the one who left, or being the one who was left behind. That hot, muggy August day had been the first chance I'd had to find out. It was the first time *I* got to get on an airplane and go somewhere new.

My tears had been real. I was leaving behind my parents, my friends, and my hometown of Ithaca, New York. Not to mention my house, the farm where I worked in the summers and picked pumpkins in the fall, and all my favorite places to swim and hike. I knew what I was leaving behind, but I didn't know what was ahead of me.

This time, I hugged my parents tight, but I didn't cry, and I looked back only once to wave at them as I went through the security line. This time, I knew where I was going, and I knew I could handle it.

I think I like leaving more than being left. Much, much more, in fact.

• • •

It takes a long time to get from Ithaca, New York, to Rexburg, Idaho. I had to change planes twice and endure long car rides to and from the airport on either end. All of the traveling made me bored and impatient. I couldn't *wait* to get started on the new semester! Everyone always tells you that things like starting high school or going to your first dance or graduating are going to be cool. For me at least, college was the one thing that had lived up to my expectations and more.

I looked at my watch impatiently as the shuttle from the Salt Lake City Airport grumbled along the road. We still had an hour to go before I reached Rexburg. I was going to be the last one in our apartment back from the Christmas break, and I was so excited to see my roommates. I knew two of them, and the three of us had already become close. Our fourth roommate had moved out at the semester break (she had gotten married), and so we were going to have a new roommate. I was looking forward to meeting her and having another close-to-perfect semester at BYU–Idaho.

. . .

When I had been home during the holidays, I went to dinner one night at Joel and Andrea Hammond's house. Joel and Andrea had been my seminary teachers my senior year of high school, and after my graduation, they had also become my friends. Andrea was the one who had helped me find my roommates; one of them, Noelle, was her cousin. They'd needed another person for their apartment after someone bailed out, and I had been only too happy to sign up. It was nice to have some kind of connection to start out with, even if it was a small one, and Noelle and her friend Liz had turned out to be lots of fun.

"How is school going?" Andrea asked me.

"Perfect," I told her. It's not a word I use very often, but no other word could describe how college had been so far. "I honestly couldn't love it more. My ward is friendly, I like most of my classes, and my roommates are the best. I'm so glad you told me about Noelle and Liz. They're awesome."

"It doesn't sound like you're having any of the usual freshman homesickness," Joel said.

"I did for the first day or two," I admitted. "But it didn't last longer than that."

"That's great," Andrea said. She sounded enthusiastic, but I could tell her mind had wandered to something else.

Joel could too. "What is it, Andrea? I promise, everything should be ready in a couple of minutes." Joel was cooking dinner, and I guess he thought she was worried about how the meal would turn out.

"Oh, I know. You're a great cook. I was just wondering about Steve. What's going on with him lately?"

"You'd probably know more than I would," I told her, not

entirely truthfully. Steve had also been in our seminary class, and he and I were friends. Sometimes, I felt like we had the potential of being something more than just friends. I think Andrea agreed with me, because she always asked about him. "I haven't seen Steve since last summer. He and his family went to Florida to visit his grandparents for the holidays, so I haven't seen him this whole break."

"Oh," Andrea said. "I'd forgotten they weren't going to be in town."

"We saw him at Thanksgiving," Joel said. "He seemed to be doing well. He's almost ready to turn in his mission papers, but I bet you knew that already."

I nodded. I didn't see Steve all that often, but we did call and text each other pretty frequently. In fact, he'd texted me from Florida only a few minutes before I'd left to drive to Joel and Andrea's for dinner. He told me he'd found a pineapple tie in Florida and wanted to know if I thought it would be appropriate for a missionary. I'd written back "no." Then he'd asked if a Mickey Mouse tie would work. I told him "no" again. Then he accused me of being picky. I wrote back that he should try to find a Disney princess tie because *that* would be appropriate.

You see how our relationship is. Maybe there's not that much potential after all.

"I've been thinking I want to do something different this summer," I told Joel and Andrea. "All the guys my age are going on missions. All I'm doing is coming home and working at the farm again and then going back to school—which I love—but I think I'm up for a new challenge."

"I might have an idea for you," Andrea told me. "Would you want to live in Seattle for a couple of months?"

I raised my eyebrows. I'd never been to that part of the country, and now that I knew I could make it on my own, I wanted to see more of the world. "Tell me more."

"I might have a job lead for you. I did an internship at a cancer research center the summer after I graduated, and I heard they're looking for some interns again this year. They have some positions that last the whole summer, and some that are only from mid-April to mid-June."

"*Really?* That would be perfect." I could have a new adventure and still get to go back home for part of the summer. Despite my whining, I did look forward to working on the farm again and seeing my old friends.

"I'll e-mail you the link to the application. It would look great on a resumé, especially in your field. Not that that's the only reason to apply." Andrea looked thoughtful. "Rent can get expensive in the city. But I bet you could live with my family. I'll ask them and see what they think."

"Do you think they'd mind?"

"I think they'd love it."

"Thanks," I told her sincerely. This was turning out perfectly. I was becoming a real world traveler.

The timer beeped in the kitchen, and Joel and Andrea went to bring in the food. I offered to help, but they told me to stay where I was and relax. I took a peek at the cell phone in my pocket. There was a message there. It was from Steve. I smiled and resisted the temptation to look at it right then.

When I checked the message later, I started laughing. Steve had sent a picture of himself, standing in a gift shop wearing a Disney princess tie. Those Disney marketing people think of everything. I wished I hadn't waited until I got home to check the message. Joel and Andrea would have gotten a kick out of the picture.

For a minute, I was tempted to keep it as the background on my phone, but I didn't.

• • •

The shuttle was just pulling into Rexburg when a message from Steve popped up. This time, it was a text message. "Turned in my mission papers today. I wanted you to know. Good luck with the new roommate."

I wished again that our paths had crossed over the holidays. It had been a long time since we'd seen each other.

I wrote him back quickly while I waited for the shuttle to drive to my stop. "Congratulations. Good luck to you too. Talk to you soon." I didn't know what else to say, but I was glad for the connection and wanted to keep our friendship going. Steve and I were both heading for lots of new adventures in our lives, and I wondered how long we would keep sharing them with each other. I hoped it would be for a long time.

As I lugged my bag up the stairs to our apartment, I could see the lights on in the kitchen. I peered through the window, where I could see three people—my roommates—sitting at the table. I opened the door on the new semester.

CHAPTER 4

JANUARY

Addie Sherman

I'd been putting it off all day, but it was time to face the music. I unfolded the English paper Mrs. Bryant had handed me after class and looked at the grade. I was hoping it would be a B, or maybe even a B+, since I'd spent hours on this stupid, stupid, *stupid* paper.

It was a C.

Of course it was a C. I had to maintain a "B" average if I wanted to be able to keep snowboarding. I'd gotten the same stupid C on all of my English papers the last few weeks, whether I tried hard or not. A smart person would have recognized this fact and quit trying, but I was obviously not a smart person.

What was I going to tell my parents?

Was I going to tell my parents?

I might be able to get away without saying anything for awhile. Maybe until I could figure out some way to get better grades. My parents probably wouldn't ask me about the paper. They assumed I had school under control the way my brothers always had. Although they were crazy and goofy and didn't always apply themselves, my brothers had always gotten decent grades. Which was unfair, but typical. Eric even finished high school early and headed off to college at seventeen.

If I didn't tell my parents about my grade, it would buy me some more snowboarding time.

My parents and I don't fight. We also don't talk. It's not that we hate each other. We seem to be at a stalemate. We're not close like we used to be when I was younger. It's like we're in some kind of parent/child relationship limbo.

I started walking down the hall. As I got close to the doors leading to the parking lot, I made my decision. I crumpled up the paper and threw it in the trash can—the same one where I'd also thrown the flyer announcing the stupid Holiday Formal.

"Addie, wait," someone called, a voice I recognized. Cody. I turned around. He was jogging toward me.

"What's the weather forecast?" I asked him. "I didn't have time to check this morning."

"Two inches of snow last night, clear with scattered showers tonight. Looks like the *five* of us will have a good time." There was a mischievous glint in his eye.

"The *five* of us?" I asked.

"Didn't you hear? Rob is bringing his girlfriend."

I hadn't heard anyone refer to Brook as Rob's girlfriend yet, even though they'd been out a few times since the Holiday Formal, but the fact that she was coming boarding with us seemed proof enough.

"You're kidding me. He's bringing her *snowboarding?*"

Cody laughed. "That's what I said. Rob says she really wants to learn. He must have it bad."

"He didn't even ask any of us." I groaned. For a minute, I toyed with the idea of backing out. I didn't want to spend the whole afternoon watching Rob and Brook flirt with each other. It was hard enough that he was dating someone; the only good part about it was that she didn't go to our school, so I didn't have to see the whole relationship develop in front of my eyes every day.

"I guess he doesn't have to since it's his car," Cody pointed out. The two of us reached my car and started gathering our equipment. I'd given Cody a ride that morning, and the car was crammed full of our things.

"Well, maybe I won't go," I said, knowing even as I said it how stupid and petty I sounded.

"Why?" asked Cody. "Do you hate her?" Luckily, neither he nor Sam had ever figured out that I'd had a crush on Rob.

"No. She's nice, I guess. It's just the idea of bringing someone who hasn't ever even boarded before . . ." I sighed.

"No kidding. I hope Rob knows that we're not all going to stick around on the beginner hill with her."

"I'm sure he doesn't want us to anyway." I could picture Rob helping Brook up when she fell, the two of them laughing, holding onto each other longer than necessary. I bit my lip. Yeah, I would not be sticking around the beginner hill either. No point in torturing myself.

A car horn startled me. Rob leaned out of his window, grinning. "Come on, you guys. Let's get going." Sam was already sitting in the front seat, so Cody and I strapped our gear to the roof and then climbed in the backseat.

"This is going to be a tight fit when we pick up Brook," Cody muttered to me. "You can bet she'll get the front seat."

When we pulled up to Brook's high school, she was already standing out front and waving at us. We parked next to the curb and Sam hopped out, joining Cody and me in the back. The three of us were pretty cramped. I had a feeling our days of riding shotgun were over, and that the front seat was now permanently Brook's. I was willing to bet she wasn't going to pay her share of gas money either, but I put on a smile and tried to look friendly. I had nothing against her, really, except that Rob liked her.

"Hey, Addie!" Brook called out, climbing into the car. "Hey, guys!" She waved to Sam and Cody. The three of us were sitting shoulder to shoulder, wedged in like Wal-Mart shoppers caught in the door at the 4:00 AM Day-After-Thanksgiving Sale.

"Sorry I'm making everyone so squished in the back." Brook turned around to give us an apologetic smile.

"It wouldn't be such a problem if Addie wasn't so fat," joked Cody.

Guys don't seem to realize that even if you're skinny, joking about your weight in front of you still isn't okay if you're a girl.

Sam looked over at me, saw my expression, and tried to change the subject. "So, Brook, have you ever been snowboarding before?"

"No." She made a worried face. "I'm scared I'll be terrible. But I figured out fast that if I ever wanted to spend a Friday night hanging out with Rob, I'd better learn how to snowboard." She and Rob exchanged smiles. Cody rolled his eyes, and I started grinning. Sam shot us both a look, so I folded my arms and stared straight ahead as we pulled out of the parking lot.

Big mistake. Staring straight ahead between the two front seats meant that I got to see Brook and Rob holding hands, talking to each other, giving each other little looks and secret smiles. It only took about two seconds of that before I decided to look out Cody's window instead.

"What are you staring at?" Cody demanded.

"I'm looking out your window."

"She just can't get over how hot you are, Cody," Rob said from the front seat, turning enough to flash a teasing smile at me.

"Great," said Cody. "Try to control yourself, Addie. There are people around."

"Don't flatter yourself," I told him.

"No, seriously," Cody said. "We could have Sam sit between us if this is going to be a problem."

"I don't think so," Sam said. "I'm staying right where I am. Addie smells a lot better than you do."

Rob and Brook were laughing as though the exchange was the

funniest thing they'd ever heard in their lives. Then Rob leaned over to whisper to Brook, and she laughed even harder.

I knew they probably weren't making fun of me, but it was easy to imagine that they were.

"Here," Sam said, handing me his iPod. "Listen to this song. It's awesome. Trust me. You're going to want to hear it more than once."

Grateful for the diversion, I popped the earphones into my ears and started listening, closing my eyes. Sam tapped me on the shoulder after a few minutes and raised his eyebrows at me. I gave him a thumbs-up to show that I liked the song (I did), and he leaned back in his seat, satisfied. I closed my eyes again and listened to the music, ignoring Cody when he reached over me to steal some of Sam's food.

Sam didn't ask for his iPod back, so I kept it. I stayed that way for the rest of the ride—eyes closed, insulated in the middle of music no one else could hear.

• • •

When I felt the car slow down, I finally opened my eyes. No big surprise—we were pulling into the parking lot of the main slope, the one with the bunny hill for beginners. Usually, we go straight over to the best hill, Blackhawk, but it looked like we were going to have to take the shuttle over there so Rob could teach Brook how to board on the easy slope. Perfect.

The song I was listening to wasn't over yet, so I kept the earphones in while everyone around me started talking and getting their gear together. I had to wait for Sam and Cody to get out before I could leave the car, so I closed my eyes to concentrate on the lyrics at the end of the song. When I opened my eyes a few seconds later, I realized everyone was looking at me. I felt a flush of embarrassment in my face.

"She's still in her own world." Sam reached over and pulled out one of the earphones, gently. "So? You ready to get boarding, or what? Let's catch the shuttle over to Blackhawk."

"Why don't you guys hang out with us for a few runs?" Rob asked, pulling Brook's rented board out for her.

The looks on Cody's and Sam's faces were priceless. "Um," Sam started, but Cody broke in. "You don't need us. We'll just get in the way. We'll head over to Blackhawk and meet you back here in a couple of hours."

"No, Addie, don't leave me!" Brook said, and she looked genuinely nervous. "I was hoping you'd help me out at the beginning. Rob says you're one of the best around, and I know I'm going to need a lot of help."

Oh, great. I couldn't leave her after that. I'm not a jerk. I looked over at Cody and Sam for support. Cody was grinning away at my situation. Sam managed to keep a straight face.

"Okay," I said. "No problem."

To my surprise, Sam and Cody stuck around the hill too. They didn't hang out with Rob and Brook and me, but at least they didn't abandon me entirely. Brook wasn't any better or any worse than most first-time snowboarders. Lots of falling and getting up, but at least she was paying attention to what we were telling her and genuinely trying to learn. She boarded goofy foot (with her right foot in front), which is how I board, so I showed her how to turn and stop. We practiced for awhile at the bottom of the run, hiking up a small hill and then going down again.

"I think I'm ready. Do you think I can try it from the top?" She was asking me, not Rob.

"Go for it. That's the only way to find out if you're ready. Give it a shot. You'll fall, but it's okay. Falling comes with the territory."

She fell plenty. It took us forever to get down the mountain. I would go first and wait for her at the bottom of each little hill on the run, and Rob would stay with her and help her up when she fell. Then, when they reached me, I'd give her some pointers about what I'd noticed from watching her, and off we'd go again. It was a pretty good arrangement because I could at least board for a minute or two uninterrupted instead of stopping each time Brook wiped out, and she and Rob got to laugh and flirt when he'd help her up each time she fell. At least I didn't have to be right there for it.

"When you try to stop, you're still cutting too hard," I told her. "You need to be less abrupt. You still want to do it fast, but not too fast or you'll fall over."

"But you always stop so fast and turn so sharp, and you don't fall."

"I've been doing this for awhile. You'll get there."

"Thanks, Addie. I'm beginning to wonder." She took a deep breath. "You go ahead."

I took off, then stood at the bottom of the last swell of the slope, waiting for her to come down. Out of nowhere, Sam whooshed to a stop next to me. Together, we looked up at the pink splotch that was Brook. She fell almost immediately, despite what I'd told her minutes before. But she was going so slow it wasn't even much of a fall. She sort of tipped over almost in slow motion. I laughed.

"Be nice," Sam told me.

"I'm *being* nice. I've been on this stupid slope for the last hour helping her while you guys go on run after run after run."

"All right," Sam said. "But you could be *nicer.* You keep leaving her up there with Rob and going down as fast as you can, and now you're standing here laughing at her. She might learn more if you stuck right with her."

"She's not really here to learn how to board, Sam. She's here to hang out with Rob." Rob helped her up from her fall and the wind carried their laughter down to us. I sighed. "I'm not trying to be mean. Cody's been laughing too. Get after him, why don't you?"

"Cody's hopeless." Sam grinned. "He's always kidding around. But you're not hopeless. You're willing to help people out."

"Not always." I was thinking of the time Rob had asked me for help in asking Brook to the dance.

"You were my first friend when I moved into the neighborhood.

Everyone else was mocking my bowl haircut and my braces, but you invited me to play basketball at your house with you and your brothers and all your friends."

I started smiling, remembering Sam when he was eight years old and first came to our elementary school. I'd been seven, but even then I could tell he needed a friend.

"That *was* nice of me, wasn't it?" I joked.

"You're always trying to include the outsider. That's one of the best things about you." Sam looked at the expression on my face. "But it's obvious you'd rather be somewhere else."

"Well, I *would* rather be somewhere else. And besides, Brook's not an outsider. She's making *me* feel like the outsider." I looked up to where she and Rob were standing and flirting—again—before they continued their way down the mountain. "But I don't have anything against her."

"You just don't like losing your position as the only girl in this group," Sam teased.

"Oh, please." I was unable to keep the edge out of my voice. "None of you even notice that I am a girl."

"I've noticed," Sam said. I turned away from Rob and Brook to say some kind of comeback, but he wasn't smiling or laughing. I didn't know what to think.

Was he teasing me? What if he wasn't? Sam was great, but he wasn't the right guy. *Rob* was the right guy, even if he was standing up there on the mountain with someone else.

Cody skidded to a stop next to us before I could speak. "Let's get out of here," he said. "I told Rob on my way down we were going to catch the shuttle over to Blackhawk. He's fine with that. Brook said to thank you again for your help, Addie." I looked back up the mountain to where they stood. Brook started waving at us. I waved back.

As we waited for the shuttle, Cody was grumbling. "We spent half the night on the easy slopes. What's happened to Friday?"

That, I told myself, *is the question of the night.*

• • •

We were all worn out on the way home. Cody and Sam and I were tired from burning up the runs on Blackhawk for two hours. Rob and Brook were tired from falling and flirting, I'd bet. They murmured to each other quietly and held hands in the front seat.

I had to sit in the back between Cody and Sam again. Sam was making sure our arms didn't touch and was crammed almost right up against the window. Great. I wondered if he thought I was suddenly going to have a crush on *him.* Cody, on the other hand, didn't seem worried about my falling in love with him. He was exhibiting his usual disregard for personal space and periodically leaned over me to talk to Rob and Brook in the front.

I hated that I was turning back into "shy" Addie again, not daring to talk in the one place and group where I'd felt safe for the past year.

One thing I remembered from *The Hunchback of Notre Dame,* the book I'd written my C-worthy paper on, was the idea of sanctuary. I guess in the Middle Ages, places like churches were supposed to be safe for people who needed protection from the outside world. Even if sanctuaries didn't always work the way they were supposed to (especially not for Quasimodo and Esmeralda), I liked the idea of it—a place where you could call out "Sanctuary!" and claim peace and protection from everything. Fridays and snowboarding had been my sanctuary. But it seemed like that was gone too. I'd practically screamed it to the mountains that day, but it hadn't been the same.

"What are you thinking about?" Sam asked me.

I didn't want to tell him. "Nothing. Just school."

If the mountains weren't my safe place anymore, then what was?

• • •

I came home to a dark house, except for the one light in my parents' room. My mom would want to come down and talk to me about how my night had been, what I'd had for dinner, how every-thing had gone. Usually, I disappointed her because my answers were the same every Friday night. ("The snow was decent. I brought a sandwich. Everything went great.")

Tonight, though, I could tell her about Brook and Rob and Sam, and how everything was changing, and nothing was fair.

But even thinking about going into all the details made me so tired that I knew I wouldn't say anything. It would be one thing if she'd listen and nod and say, "That stinks." But I knew she wouldn't. She'd try to tell me how everything would be okay, and how I was beautiful, and that any guy who got to date me would be lucky. I didn't have the energy for that conversation.

I unlocked the door and headed for the kitchen, leaving my snowboard in the entryway. I knew exactly what I wanted to eat. It was sugary and chocolatey and creamy and horribly unhealthy. There was one Hostess cupcake left in the pantry, and it was going to be mine.

Sometimes I love not having any brothers at home anymore.

In the kitchen, I hit the light switch nearest the sink, pulled out the trash can and yanked the red, white, and blue hat I'd worn that day out of my coat pocket. It had been even unluckier than the ugly brown-and-orange one I'd worn the day I found out Rob wanted to ask Brook to the Holiday Formal. "See you later," I told the hat.

"Why are you throwing my old beanie in the trash?" asked a voice from the pantry.

I shrieked and turned around, clutching the beanie to my heart. My older brother Dave stepped out of the pantry, eating the last Hostess cupcake. Figures.

"Dave, what are you doing here? It's late."

"I've been waiting for you. I need to talk to you." He dropped into a chair, shoving the last bite in his mouth. He looked exhausted. Something was going on. I decided not to give him a hard time about the cupcake.

"What's up? Where's Avery?" Avery is Dave's wife, my sister-in-law. The two of them had announced at Christmas that they were expecting a baby in June.

"She's at home. I came over to talk to you."

"Well, here I am," I said, trying to move things along. What could he want to talk to me about? I dropped the beanie on the counter.

"We had a rough day today," Dave said slowly, picking up my hat and turning it in his hands.

I suspected this could take awhile. I grabbed a granola bar and sat down too.

"Avery had some trouble, and we went to the doctor. It looks like she's going to have to be on strict bed rest for a long time, maybe even the rest of the pregnancy. The doctor says she can get up only to go to the bathroom. That's it. The rest of the time she has to be lying down."

"Oh, man, Dave. I'm sorry." I was, but I still didn't know what it had to do with me. Was Dave trying to have a heart-to-heart about the situation? My mom would be a better person for that.

Right on cue, she came into the room. "Addie, you're back. Dave, did you tell Addie what's going on?"

"Yeah." Dave turned back to me. "We're trying to figure out a way to do this bed rest thing and keep us both in school and me working. We need the money." Dave worked the evening shift at the Lighthouse, one of the fanciest restaurants in our suburb of Seattle, and he made a lot of money in tips. "I don't want Avery to be alone all day, in case anything happens or if she needs help. I mean, she's not even supposed to get up to make herself lunch. We've figured out a plan for the mornings when I'm at school, but that still leaves the afternoons when I'm at work." He paused and looked at me. "So, Addie, I'll pay you if you'll come over after school a couple of days a week for a few hours. Avery and I have been talking about it, and we think it's our best plan. What do you think?"

"You need me to babysit Avery?" I said, and in spite of myself, I started to smile at the idea. I could not imagine anything either of us would enjoy less. My sister-in-law and I don't fight, but we also don't hang out. Or talk. Or do anything really except say hello to each other. It's just that we're so different. Avery is quieter than most people in my family, but she also states her mind when she really feels like it, and she has a lot of inner self-confidence, something I don't have. Plus, she's old. She's in college and having a baby. That's a whole different ball game than being in high school.

"I don't know if that will work," my mom butted in. "Addie needs her time to study. Especially for English. I could come over instead."

"We thought the best way for this to not be a burden on everyone would be to divide it up," Dave said. "Addie could come a couple of days, and then maybe you and Avery's mom could come a couple of days. And remember, Mom, Avery's an English major. She could help Addie with her homework and all that."

My mom looked reflective. "That's true . . ."

"So what do you say?" Dave looked at me eagerly.

How could I say no? I'm not made of stone. "Okay, okay. I'll help you. But you don't need to pay me. In fact, I won't do it if you pay me." I knew they needed the money.

"That's way too generous of you," he said, but I could see the relief in his eyes. Things were tight with both of them in school, and now Avery wouldn't be working part-time.

"You'll just have to name the baby after me."

"You don't think one Adelaide Sherman is enough in this world?" he joked, but then he gave me a hug. "This is a huge load off my mind, Addie. Thank you." He handed the beanie back to me.

I smiled at him because I didn't want him to know that I was feeling the opposite way. I felt like one more thing had been added to an already too-full plate. School, snowboarding, Rob—none of it was going well. I couldn't imagine that babysitting my pregnant sister-in-law would be any different.

But Sam's comment about being nice still stung. Even if I didn't have anything else going for me—guys, school, whatever—I still wanted to be a nice person. Or, at least, I wanted to have people think of me as being a nice person. Most of the time.

When I finally lay down in bed after talking logistics with Dave about my coming over the next week, I looked up at the ceiling. I remembered Rob and Brook holding hands in the dark as we drove home, and the way the headlights of the passing cars lit up their faces as they talked. I felt lonelier than ever. And I didn't care much about being a nice person right then, but instead wanted to be one who didn't hurt so much inside.

CHAPTER 5

JANUARY

Sam Choi

"You look handsome," Mom told me, straightening my tie.

"You look stupid," Alex told me, walking through the living room on his way to the kitchen.

"Alex!" Mom said. "Knock it off. He looks *handsome,* and remember, you'll be doing the same thing in a few years."

"Don't worry about defending me, Mom. I'll take care of him later."

I wore a white shirt and tie every week to church, but one of my Christmas gifts had been a suit. Mom insisted I wear it to go on splits with the missionaries. She was also after me to cut my hair, even though it wasn't that long compared to other guys at school. I wasn't about to cut it just because she wanted me to.

I know this sounds like I don't like my mom. But I do. She's cool. But when she gets excited, she goes full steam ahead and assumes everyone else is along for the ride. In the case of my future, my mission, and my college plans, she was trying to back off and leave the decisions up to me. But it wasn't coming easy to her.

She thought she was being discreet about it, but I knew what she *really* wanted. She was hoping I would go on my mission right after my birthday in October. She was hoping the mission call would be to Korea, or at least Korean-speaking. She was hoping I would decide to go to BYU when I got back. And she probably had hopes about my getting married and having kids, and going to medical school and curing cancer.

Mom was already taking off, and I wasn't even at the airport. Scratch that. I didn't even have my bags packed.

I'd been right about the wedding being a great distraction. Mom had so much to do to get ready for the wedding that she was totally focused on that (except for this going-on-splits-with-the-missionaries thing), and Alex and I were getting away with murder. Well, not murder, but we were eating a lot of pizza and slacking off. And she hadn't even mentioned our painting the living room yet. Alex said if she'd lost her coupon, we didn't have to honor it.

The doorbell rang. "That must be Elder Murray," Mom said.

I'd only met Elder Murray twice before: once at church and once when he and his companion came over for dinner. Elder Murray seemed like an okay guy, which was more than I could say for his companion. One of the first things out of the companion's mouth was a compliment on how well my family spoke English. Of course we speak English. All of us were born in America. When Dad politely mentioned that fact, it was quiet for a minute, and Elder Murray gave his companion a look that could kill and changed the subject. But his companion still didn't get the hint. Later, he asked if the dinner we were eating was authentic Chinese food. For one thing, we're Korean-American, not Chinese-American, and for another thing, it was a Thai recipe that Mom got from a friend at work. The guy was a real cultural expert.

I was glad I wasn't going on splits with the companion. I didn't even remember his name because Alex and I, inspired by a *Simpsons* episode where they call Nelson "Smellson," had called him Elder

Smellder until Mom and Dad made us stop, saying we weren't being respectful.

"So, have you ever been on splits before?" Elder Murray asked me.

"No," I admitted. "What do you do?" I'd assumed we would be knocking on doors.

"Today, we're going to visit a referral. It's a family that the Johnsons know." The Johnsons were a family in our ward and they were always bringing friends to church and activities. I didn't know them very well because all their kids were younger than I was.

"Okay." That didn't sound too bad. In fact, it sounded way better than knocking on doors or trying to talk to people in the streets. I'd driven by when the missionaries were doing that, and I always felt bad for them. They looked kind of pathetic. They were standing there in their suits and ties and talking away a mile a minute, and you could usually tell that the person they were talking to wanted to get away as soon as possible.

Sometimes the person they were talking to was arguing with them. It all seemed potentially humiliating.

Elder Murray was still talking. "This family that we're going to see—the Smiths—have a couple of kids. They live across the street from the Johnsons and wanted to find out some more about the Church."

"Okay," I said again.

I think missionary work must be like any other talent. Some people have it, some don't. I didn't think it was going to be one of my talents.

Our ward boundaries are big, so we rode bikes over to the Smiths' house instead of walking. When I pulled my bike out of the garage, I realized I needed to dust it off or I would have a big dirt spot on the back of my new suit. I grabbed a rag from a pile and ran it over the seat. It had been a long time since I'd ridden my bike. I used to love it, but then I got a driver's license and started snow-boarding.

I followed Elder Murray along the streets. He was wearing a helmet, and too late, I realized I should have grabbed mine. Then again, who knew if it would even fit? Mom would argue it wouldn't, and she'd try to use that as another reason for me to cut my hair.

It wasn't raining, but the clouds were still dark gray, and the grass on the lawns was matted, more brown than green. The air was cold, but it wasn't too bad. It felt exactly the way February should feel in Seattle.

The ride over to the Johnsons' house was familiar too. I almost didn't have to think. I must have stored the route in my brain when I was riding as a kid. I wasn't surprised when I bumped over the big crack from the roots of the Carpenter's tree, and I knew when the sidewalks would turn from smooth cement into some weird, pebbly rock material that must have been popular back in the seventies or eighties when the subdivision had been built. Alex and I used to start yelling right before we hit that part so our voices would go "uh-uh-uh," and we'd laugh at how stupid we sounded.

I also knew where the curbs were that you could jump and get some serious air, but I didn't think Elder Murray was dying to know about that, so I didn't tell him. I followed him along and avoided the puddles like he did. Gotta keep the suit clean.

We stopped at the Smiths' house and wheeled our bikes over to the side, locking them up to the lamppost. There was a basketball hoop in the driveway and a kid's scooter lying on the grass. It seemed like a friendly place.

"So what happens now?" I asked Elder Murray as we walked toward the door. "Do we teach them a lesson or something?"

"When I spoke to Mrs. Smith, she said they just want to ask us some questions about the Church. They want it to be informal. So that's what we'll do—see what they want to ask about and go from there. And of course I brought a Book of Mormon, although I wouldn't be surprised if the Johnsons have already given them one."

"All right." I hung back as Elder Murray knocked on the door. Even though I knew they weren't going to kick us off their property, and even though I knew they were expecting us, I still felt nervous.

Mr. Smith answered the door. He was wearing glasses and a polo shirt and looked like every other youngish dad around here who works at Microsoft or someplace like it. "Come on in," he said, stepping back and shaking our hands as we entered. "Thanks for coming."

"It's our pleasure," Elder Murray said. Mrs. Smith and two kids appeared around the corner. After all the introductions, we followed them into the living room.

"We've talked to the Johnsons about a lot of topics related to the Mormon church, but they thought we should also talk to you," Mrs. Smith said. "They said this could be an informal visit and that we didn't have to have lessons right away."

"Of course. What questions can we answer for you?" Elder Murray asked.

"Well, we wanted to know what you believe the answers are to the big questions. You know, what happens when we die? The Johnsons say that you believe families are together even after death."

Elder Murray outlined the plan of salvation, and he did it well. I was impressed. He asked if I had anything to add. I didn't. I was trying to keep myself from bouncing my foot up and down the way I usually do when I'm uncomfortable and trying to sit still. If I couldn't add to the discussion, at least I could try not to distract from it.

Mr. Smith asked the next question. "We've noticed the Johnsons don't drink or smoke. Is that a rule?"

Elder Murray briefly explained the Word of Wisdom, and then he turned to me. "What about you, Brother Choi? Have you had any experiences with the Word of Wisdom you'd like to share?"

Definitely not, I thought. "Um, not really."

It went on and on like that. Elder Murray kept trying to pass the ball to me, and I kept dropping it. I did answer one question. Mrs. Smith asked how other kids my age acted around me when they found out I was a member of the Church.

"Some of them think it's weird," I said. "But mostly they leave me alone about it. They get used to it. Once in awhile, someone wants to talk to me about it, which is always cool."

After that, though, the questions were about Joseph Smith and baptism, and I kept my mouth shut. The discussion ended with Elder Murray bearing his testimony. I liked that part. I could tell the family did too. His testimony was quiet and short and heartfelt.

When he finished, Elder Murray turned to me one final time. "Do you have anything you want to say, Brother Choi?"

I didn't. "No, that's all right."

He paused for a second, waiting. Then he asked me if I would offer a prayer before we left.

That I could do. "All right," I said, and I bowed my head.

• • •

"You can talk when we're on splits, you know," Elder Murray told me as we pedaled along my street.

"I know." I felt stupid. "I didn't know what to say."

"Now you'll have an idea for next time."

"Right." *No way is there going to be a next time,* I thought. We reached my driveway, so I thanked Elder Murray and went inside. I was hoping to get upstairs and change my clothes and just breathe for a minute before I had to talk to my parents, but Mom caught me before I had the chance.

She had a bunch of those paint sample cards in her hands. Uh-oh. She hadn't forgotten about the Christmas gift after all. "How was it?"

Sometimes it's better and easier to just tell people what they want to hear.

"Awesome," I said.

JANUARY

Caterina Giovanni

One of my favorite things about living in an all-girl apartment is that you can act stupid if you want to. Your parents aren't there to tell you to grow up, and there aren't any guys around to impress. No one is going to look at you weird if you're being crazy or if you have an attack of the giggles that's impossible to stop.

That's what was happening to us. Liz and I had just witnessed Noelle's attempt to lip-sync and choreograph a dance to one of the worst songs in the world: "Big Girls Don't Cry" by Fergie. Noelle is tall and uncoordinated and doesn't worry about what people think of her, which of course makes them like her even more. She was wearing her so-bad-it's-funny purple velour sweats, and she looked like Barney the Dinosaur trying to do interpretive dance. She was really hamming it up during the line in the song about a child missing her blanket—which I think is a stupid lyric—and that's when Liz and I completely lost it. I love my roommates.

When Liz and I finally caught our breath, we tried to give Noelle some feedback. It wasn't very constructive, but at least it was honest.

"Not that song," I gasped.

"Not that dance," added Liz. Liz is tall too, with long, almost-black hair and blue eyes. The combination is lethal for guys. They're always wandering over to our apartment trying to find out if she's around. She and Noelle have been best friends since middle school, but they are great about including me.

Noelle pretended to be mad. "Fine, then. You guys come up with a plan." She flopped down on one of the standard-issue apartment denim couches. (Where do you get denim couches, anyway? I'd never seen them until I moved to Idaho, but Noelle and Liz told me there must be some denim couches in New York, too, but that I must not know where to shop.)

"How about 'It's Raining Men'?" Liz suggested, and that set us all laughing again.

The front door opened, and Jenna, our new roommate, walked in. "What are you guys doing?" she asked, looking at the three of us.

"We're working on our performance for the ward activity in two weeks, the lip-sync," Liz said.

Jenna still looked blank.

I tried to remind her. "You know, the one they mentioned in church last Sunday?"

"Oh, yeah." She just stood in the doorway. She didn't plop down on the couch or join in or anything.

I was worried she was feeling left out. It would be hard to be the new one when all of the rest of us knew each other. I wanted to let her know that she was a part of us too. "We're trying to figure out our song. What do you want to do?"

"Oh, whatever. It doesn't matter." She shrugged and left, wandering toward the room she shared with me.

Liz and Noelle and I exchanged looks. Didn't she want to be a part of it? Did we need to be more explicit with our invitation?

"Doesn't she know this is supposed to be an apartment thing?" Noelle asked.

"I think she knows," I said. "I'll go ask."

I went into our room. Jenna was sitting at the desk, typing on her laptop. "Hey, Jenna. You're going to do this lip-sync with us, right?"

She hesitated. "Well, the thing is, I'm not even sure I can make it that night. You guys go ahead and plan it without me."

"Are you positive?"

"Yeah. If I find out I'll be around, I'll learn the dance from you later."

"All right."

Jenna turned back to her computer and continued typing. I felt that weird pause at the end of a conversation when you don't know someone and aren't sure what just happened. Was she feeling left out? Should I try harder to convince her to join us? Was she annoyed that I'd even come in and asked?

Oh, well. Whatever. She'd feel more comfortable around us as time passed. She'd realize she was lucky to have been assigned to the coolest apartment ever.

I went back to the living room and told Noelle and Liz what had happened. "She said to go ahead without her. She doesn't think she can make it to the lip-sync thing anyway."

"Oh, okay." We all looked at each other.

"She doesn't know us yet," Noelle said.

"To know us is to love us," I agreed.

"Focus, people," Liz said. "We still need to think of a song. What about 'You Don't Bring Me Flowers Anymore'?"

We all started laughing again. I didn't know if Jenna could hear us or not, but a few minutes later she came back through the living room and waved good-bye on her way out.

• • •

It meant a lot to me at the beginning of the year when Liz and Noelle were willing to include me in everything. They'd been friends before I came along, and it would have been easy for them to just stay a duo. But it hadn't been long before we were all close. The three of us hoped—or assumed—that it would be the same with Jenna. We wanted to get to know her, and we invited her to everything we did, but she never said yes. She was friendly enough, but I couldn't see how we were going to move from being acquaintances to being friends if we never hung out.

I should have had faith in the power of family home evening, because eventually that was what brought us together. Actually, I should have had faith in the power of a potential family home evening disaster. That's what truly bonds you.

Jenna came in the door one Monday night to find us frantically putting something together for FHE at the last minute. The stress level must have been high, because she stopped and asked us what was going on.

"We're trapped," Liz told her.

"By what?"

"By FHE," Noelle explained. "The guys who are in charge of it this week called and asked if everyone could meet over here tonight. A pipe in their apartment burst, their place flooded, and they're stressed out trying to clean it up."

"So Cate said yes, and then went ahead and told them that we would plan an activity too. Because, of course, they had left that until the last possible minute and didn't have any ideas for it." Liz looked at her watch. "We have twenty minutes before the other apartment is supposed to show up here."

Everyone looked at me.

"Well, they're our friends, and they were in trouble," I said defensively.

"And they're cute," Liz informed Jenna.

"Especially Chase," I agreed.

I expected Jenna to nod and then go into her room, but she sat down on the couch. "What do you think you're going to do?"

I wondered why she was helping. Was it because we'd said the guys were cute? She didn't seem to have any trouble meeting boys on her own, so I didn't think that was it. The two weekends we'd lived with her, she'd gone out both Friday and Saturday nights.

"We don't know yet."

"How about this," she said helpfully. "What if we put together some food and have everyone over for dinner? I know that's pretty basic."

"But basic is exactly what we need," Noelle agreed. "It's perfect. What could we make?"

Jenna went to the cupboard. "We could make lasagna. I've got the pre-cooked noodles and some things we can make sauce with. The only thing we need is cheese. And oregano. I'm out of oregano."

"That's okay, I have some," I told her.

"I have things for a salad," said Liz.

I called the other apartment in our FHE group and asked them to pick up some mozzarella cheese and a brownie mix.

"We're making dinner for Chase's apartment. It flooded today," I told Brett, who'd answered the phone.

"Are we going to make enough for all of us to eat?" Brett asked.

"We could. But you'd also have to pick up a couple boxes of lasagna noodles and some more lettuce. Would that be okay?"

"We can do that."

I hung up my phone. "We're all set."

• • •

Even though the four of us hadn't spent much time together, we worked well as a team. Jenna directed the lasagna-making, Liz oversaw the salads, and the rest of us helped where we were needed. We had to send one of the guys back to their apartment to bake the brownies since there was barely enough room in our oven for the lasagna, but other than that, it all went well.

Chase and his roommates were a mess when they arrived. They

were wearing dirty clothes, and you could tell they'd been working hard trying to clean up their apartment.

"You're not kidding about making us dinner, right?" Chase asked as they stepped through the door. "That would be the meanest prank ever."

"We're not kidding," Liz told him. "Can't you smell the food?"

"It was Jenna's idea," Noelle added.

"Thanks, Jenna," Chase said, and the others agreed.

She looked embarrassed. "Everyone else helped. Brett made brownies."

We all found places to sit at the table and on the couches. Twelve people made our small apartment feel crowded and busy and lively. I like it when there's a crowd, especially a happy crowd.

Everyone laughed and talked and told stories about flooding and other disasters. Even Jenna told a story about the time her parents' basement flooded, and she and her sister tried to sneak down to splash around in their floaties and swimming suits.

It was one of the best family home evenings we'd had.

• • •

After FHE, I had to go to the library to make some copies for a class assignment. Liz had to go too, so I caught a ride with her. We talked about how fun it had been to hang out with Jenna and how we hoped that the ice was finally broken.

When we got back home, I walked into my room without even thinking about knocking. It was my room, after all. I could see the light was on, so I assumed Jenna wasn't asleep.

"*Cate!*" someone squealed. Suddenly, I spotted two people sitting on Jenna's bed, two people looking slightly rumpled, two people staring at me. "Haven't you ever heard of knocking?" Jenna asked, sounding irritated.

I'm not usually afraid of confrontation. And I'm especially not afraid when I'm in the right, which I clearly was this time. Guys aren't supposed to be in our rooms ever, let alone at midnight.

But I didn't know Jenna all that well, and she'd been helpful earlier in the evening. It seemed like she was finally starting to come out of her shell. It could be that this wasn't what it looked like, and that I was jumping to conclusions somehow.

"Sorry." I stood back as they both passed me. The guy gave a halfhearted wave in my direction, and Jenna avoided eye contact with me altogether.

A few minutes later, when I was brushing my teeth at the sink in the hallway, I heard them talking in the living room. Jenna wasn't bothering to keep her voice down.

"We obviously can't hang out here. Sorry. We'll have to go somewhere else." He murmured something, and then she giggled, and the door to the apartment closed behind them.

I guess it was exactly what it looked like.

CHAPTER 7

JANUARY

Addie Sherman

There are girls who love kids and can't wait to babysit. They're the ones who nearly faint when they spot a cute baby, always ask to hold it, and then talk to it in that high-pitched voice. They're the ones who know they are definitely going to become kindergarten teachers someday.

I've never been one of those girls. I like little kids and all, but every time I babysit I get so bored I want to scream. You have to sit there and color or draw pictures, or make them snacks, or take them to the bathroom. Babysitting is one boring task after another, and sometimes the kids are whiny. So, yeah, babysitting isn't my favorite thing to do.

I knew babysitting Avery would be different, since she was an adult and everything, but I still wasn't looking forward to it at all. I must be a selfish person. When I went over to Dave and Avery's house for my first day on the job, I went reluctantly. I had a lot on my mind.

Aside from worrying about how awkward things could be with Avery, and what things might go wrong while I was there, I was also worried about school. In my backpack was enough homework to keep me busy all night. I didn't know how much longer I could keep my parents from finding out about my grades.

Adults and old people are always talking about their carefree teenage years and how they weren't all pinned down by their adult responsibilities and lives. Well, whatever. Ask any teenager how much time they get to spend doing what they actually want to do and you'll be surprised at the answer. We're jumping through hoops the same as everyone else. Maybe even more than adults. Even if they're bored or frustrated, at least they're locked into a life they got to choose at some point, not the life that other people picked for them.

• • •

I didn't have to ring the bell. Dave threw open the door when I was halfway up the walk. "Addie! Thanks for coming! You're early!"

"I am?" That wasn't intentional. I looked at my watch.

"Well, two minutes early." Dave was wearing his uniform for work: dark pants, shiny shoes, and a crisp white shirt with a dark red paisley tie. He opened the door wider. "Come on in, come on in."

I followed him back to their family room, where Avery was sitting on the couch, messing around on her laptop, looking bored.

"Hi, Addie," she said, waving at me. "Thanks for agreeing to babysit me."

"No problem." I was surprised we'd had the same thought about the definition of this job. I stood there while Dave grabbed his coat and leaned down to give her a kiss.

"I'll be back around ten," he said to Avery. "Love you. 'Bye, Ad!"

He went out the back door, and Avery and I looked at each other. We were alone. Now what? I pulled off my jacket and hung it over a chair. The two quietest people in the entire Sherman family were spending time together. At least Avery had an excuse for being quiet. She wasn't actually a Sherman, not by blood anyway. Genetically, I was supposed to be bubbly and wasn't.

"Do you want me to help you with any homework?" Avery asked. "Your mom said I should go over your English with you."

"Thanks, but I think I'm all right." I hated that they'd been talking about me and my rotten grades behind my back. No way was I going to let Avery help me. She was an English major. She'd think I was an idiot. Trying to analyze a piece of literature for me was like snowboarding for Brook—a slow and painful process.

"Are you sure? I'm still waiting for my professor to e-mail me an assignment, so I have plenty of time."

"I'm sure." I tried to change the subject. "How's work going for Dave? Didn't he get promoted to head waiter?"

Avery looked amused. "He did. And you should hear what else they have in mind for him."

"What?"

"They keep asking him to be a bartender because he's so good at talking with people. But he always tells them no. He doesn't want to be making drinks all night."

I smiled. "He doesn't know the first thing about alcohol. What would he make when they asked him to mix their drinks? Chocolate milk?"

Avery laughed. "They offered to send him to bartending class."

Picturing Dave at bartending school was even funnier. "Oh, wow."

"I know," Avery said. The conversation was dead again. Avery shifted on the couch and moved her legs, about to stand up.

"Um." I didn't think she was supposed to move. "Is there anything I can get you?"

"No, I just need to go to the bathroom."

"Do you need any help?" I hoped she didn't. Dave hadn't mentioned that.

"No, I'll be fine." She didn't look at me as she walked slowly and carefully toward the bathroom. As she disappeared from sight, I let out a sigh of relief.

This was going to be a long day, a long week, and a long few months. What were we supposed to do for all these hours? Then a thought struck me: was I supposed to cook her dinner? Dave hadn't mentioned that either.

Avery shuffled back out of the bathroom.

"Um," I said again. She looked at me. "Am I supposed to make dinner?" If I was, then I was headed to the store for some soup in a can or a frozen pizza.

"Oh, no." She settled herself carefully back on the couch. "Sorry. We should have told you about that. The restaurant always gives Dave leftovers when he works, and he brings them home for me so we eat together. I snack on these until then because I'm feeling kind of sick." She gestured to the package of crackers on the end table next to her. "But you can have whatever you want in the kitchen if you get hungry. Sorry I can't get up to cook."

"Oh, that's okay." I felt weird helping myself to the food in their cupboards, so even though I was starving, I decided to hold off on eating until I got home.

A sound came from Avery's laptop. "Oh, finally! My assignment from my professor." She turned her computer toward me. "Could you take this over to the printer at the desk for me and print the attachment so I can get started on it? I've been waiting all day for this."

"Okay." I carried her computer over to the desk, hooked up the cable to the back of the laptop, and clicked "Print."

The printer spat out her e-mail. I relayed it across the room back to Avery.

She looked it over for a minute. "This might take awhile. Do you want to watch TV or anything? I don't want you to be bored."

"No, I'm fine. I have a lot of homework to do."

"You can use the desk," she offered. "I have to stay here on this stupid couch anyway."

I looked at the desk. In addition to the printer and paper, there were also two full backpacks, an unwatered plant, a pile of old CDs, a jar of jam, three dirty plates, a set of scriptures, a light bulb, a bag of stale gummy bears, and a miniature red wagon full of crayons spilling over the wooden surface. There was no room for me at that desk.

"I think I'll go into the kitchen. Is that all right?" The kitchen was right next to the family room, so I figured she could call me if she needed me.

Avery looked up at me and then over at the desk. As if seeing it for the first time, she groaned. "What a mess. You're right, no one could study there, except Dave." Then she hesitated. "Is the kitchen table clean?"

I peeked my head around the corner. "Mostly." It had some plates and cups on it, but it wasn't nearly as cluttered as the desk. "I'll be in there if you need me."

"Sounds good." Avery was already looking back at her computer.

I sat down at the kitchen table and pulled out my assignment. Mrs. Bryant had decided to give us a take-home essay instead of a multiple-choice test. The essay was supposed to compare *Hunchback* with another depressing book we'd read that year, *The Grapes of Wrath*. She wanted us to show our ability to compare and contrast, not simply regurgitate information. That's what she told us anyway. It was quite the little speech. I'll bet the kids who want to grow up and save the world by being English teachers were super impressed and motivated.

Not me. The sad part was that I'd read both books. But my mind didn't work this way. Compare and contrast? Couldn't I just talk about the characters as themselves and what they did without having to compare them to each other? Or talk about *what* happened instead of *why* it happened?

I could hear the sound of Avery typing furiously away on her keyboard. No writer's block going on in there. For a split second, I debated going in and asking Avery for help with my assignment.

But I didn't. I looked at my paper and listened to the silence of the kitchen instead, which wasn't really silence at all but a bunch of random sounds—the humming of the fridge, the click of the furnace as it turned on, the tumbly sound of the dryer down the hall.

I started writing something, anything, to get the assignment over with so I could add another C to my collection. Why knock myself out when the result was always going to be the same?

I could still hear Avery typing on her laptop, but neither of us spoke to each other.

I was as alone here as I was everywhere else. I hadn't expected it to be different.

• • •

It was after ten o'clock when Dave walked in the door, his starched white shirt wilted and his red paisley tie loosened. He looked exhausted. "You haven't been sneaking any drinks from the bar, have you?" I joked.

He laughed and hefted a bag with the Lighthouse logo on the side. "I brought you dinner, just in case. Roasted potatoes, rosemary chicken, raspberry cheesecake."

"Thanks. That sounds awesome." My stomach growled in agreement.

"How did everything go?" He looked at Avery and then at me.

"Fine," Avery told him. "Professor Wan sent my assignment, and I've almost finished it. We've both been working on our homework all night."

"Great." Dave put the bag down on the table and walked toward her. She changed her position on the couch so he could sit next to her. He leaned down to give her a kiss. Then he looked over at me.

"Did you get all your homework done?" he asked. I shot Dave the closest thing to a glare I could muster, and he lifted his hands up in surrender. "What? Mom is going to kill me if we mess up your schoolwork."

"Dave, we have to make a deal. I'll keep coming over to help as long as no one asks me if I've done my homework."

Avery laughed from the couch.

"All right, all right. I can't afford for you to be mad at me." Dave reached over next to the couch and pulled out some TV trays. "You'll stay and eat dinner with us, right?" he asked, propping up the trays. "We have an extra tray."

"I think I'll head home. Maybe next time."

"All right. Thanks again," Dave said. Avery thanked me too.

I waved to them and headed out the door. I turned back to tell Dave I appreciated the food, when I saw him sitting next to Avery on the couch. She was stroking his hair and saying something. Whatever it was, it made Dave smile. I kept my mouth shut.

I didn't feel needed enough. That was the problem. Even today—what had I done? I hung out with Avery and printed off her assignment for her and sat around. Anyone could have done that. The one person she truly needed was Dave.

No one really needs me as Addie, just as filler. Someone to sit in the kitchen if your husband isn't around. Someone to talk to when the girl you like isn't there. Someone to hold the place of someone more important.

JANUARY

Sam Choi

I was thinking about asking Addie to the Valentine's Day dance. I'd never been big on dating, but I would be graduating soon, and I had never been to a dance with Addie. I didn't want to miss the chance.

I wasn't into doing a big, crazy extravaganza to ask a girl out. Cody and I were in agreement about that. We figured we should save all that effort for the date. It's not like it's a marriage proposal.

But I did have one rule about asking a girl out: I always asked in person. I was on my way out the door to go to Addie's house when Mom made me come back.

"Where are you going, Sam? Dinner's ready."

"All right." I went back inside. I'd try again later.

Mom and Dad were cool about giving us our freedom, but there was one rule Alex and I didn't dare break. We were supposed to be home for dinner, and we didn't mess with that, unless we had a commitment that our parents had already approved. Friday nights were the exception, although my parents always got pizza and rented a movie to entice us to stay. It was kind of sad because it used to be all of us hanging out on Friday nights, but one by one, we'd outgrown it. Even Alex had a social life. So my parents were the only ones around for the Friday night party.

But it was Thursday night, not Friday, so I couldn't get off the hook. I walked back into the kitchen.

"Could you get the butter out of the fridge?" Mom asked me.

I went to the fridge. There, stuck to the door with the plastic alphabet magnets we'd had since we were kids, were my three college acceptance letters—from BYU, the University of Washington, and Washington State. Not bad for a semi-slacker. The only school I was still waiting to hear back from was the University of Colorado.

I noticed Alex had used the plastic letters to spell something stupid, so I rearranged them before Mom found out and blamed me instead. I spelled out "Alex is a fol." We were missing the other "o" I needed to spell "fool," but it was close enough.

When I'd finished, I brought the butter to the table, where everyone was waiting. After the blessing on the food, Mom didn't waste any time. She must have seen me pause at the fridge and thought I was admiring my acceptance letters.

"So, Sam, what are you thinking these days? Do you know which university you like best? Do you want to go to college right away, or do you want to defer admission?"

Neither, Mom. "I was thinking I might work for a semester," I said. *Or for a year or two,* but I didn't say that.

Dead silence at the table. "Pass the butter," I told Alex.

"Where do you want to work?" Dad asked.

"I don't know yet. I was thinking someplace like a sporting goods store. I think I'd like that. And I could talk to Dave, Addie's brother, and see if the Lighthouse is hiring. I know he makes decent money there. I could save up a bunch."

"Don't you want to get started on your mission as soon as possible?" Mom asked. The gloves were off. She was finally going right ahead and expressing her preferences. Maybe she'd gotten sick of thinking about the wedding and decided to take a break to worry about my life instead. I wondered if she could somehow tell I wasn't sure about going and thought she needed to send me packing as soon as she could.

"It's not a bad idea to save up money," Dad said. "I did the same thing myself before I left."

"It would be good to get a semester of school under your belt, too," Mom said.

So that was her Plan B. She *really* must not like the idea of me working for awhile.

"I'm tired of school. I'll have been going for twelve years, and then I'll be studying like crazy on my mission. I want a break."

"I can see your point." Good old Mom. She was trying. I could almost see the angel and the devil sitting on her shoulders arguing it out, one of them telling her to let me choose, the other one telling her to talk me into doing what she felt was best. I didn't know which was which, though. Would the little angel really be telling her that I could make the right choice?

Alex was staring at me. "What are you thinking about? You look like an idiot."

I'd been staring off into space, thinking about imaginary angels and devils sitting on Mom's shoulders. I scooped up some more potatoes with my fork.

Mom couldn't help herself. She had to find out more. "But, if you *were* picking a college right now, which one do you think you'd choose?"

"BYU," I said, to make her happy.

"Are you just saying that to make me happy?"

She was on to me. "I don't know where I'd want to go," I admitted. "I'm having a hard time thinking about it." That was the closest I'd come to talking about the real problem.

I expected her to tell me that that was too bad and that I'd *have* to think about it, but she nodded. "I know. Big decisions aren't easy for me, either."

"Neither are little ones," Alex pointed out helpfully. "You've had those paint samples for weeks."

"I'll decide on a color soon. Then you can paint the living room for me."

I glared at Alex.

Dad caught my eye. "If you do want to talk about it, let us know."

"Right." Since I didn't even want to think about it, wanting to talk about it seemed like it would happen . . . never.

• • •

After dinner I asked Mom if I could borrow her car, and I drove over to Addie's house to ask her to the dance. I could have talked to her about it at school, but that seemed awkward, and I didn't want to wait. Once I finally make a decision, I don't have trouble acting on it.

I rang the doorbell, and Mrs. Sherman answered. "Hi, Sam! Come on in."

"Thanks."

"We got the invitation to your sister's wedding reception," she said, leading me into the family room, where Addie was sitting at the desk. "Mikey looks beautiful! They're such a cute couple. It's so wonderful that she and Ethan ended up together."

"He's a good guy," I agreed.

Addie turned away from the computer screen. "Hey, Sam. Do you remember this from last year?"

"What is it?"

"The final paper on *Hunchback*." Addie has English with Mrs. Bryant, who taught my junior English class last year. I'm in Mrs. Bryant's advanced placement English class now. Two years of the same teacher is a lot, but luckily I like Mrs. Bryant.

"Nope."

"I wish she'd give us a real test instead. I hate it when she has us write a paper in place of a test. It takes so much longer, and you have to do it at home. Plus we *already* wrote a paper about this book." Addie was all fired up. Her parents have all these rules about snowboarding and grades, and English is her hardest subject.

"She does that in our class too. What are you writing about?"

"I was thinking I'd write about the importance of sanctuary in this book, and how Quasimodo keeps trying to find safety in the church, and then in his relationships with Frollo and Esmeralda but how none of it works out, and then I was going to write about how that relates to the Joads in *The Grapes of Wrath* and how they were hoping California would be a sanctuary for them, but it didn't work out for them either." She said it all in one breath.

"And you're always saying you aren't smart," I teased her. "That's a great idea."

"It's a great *idea,* but that's all I have to say about it. I've been working on this paper for two days, and that's still the only thing I've written down. I can't turn in a one-sentence essay." She threw her copy of *Hunchback* down on the table. "This book is so depressing anyway. English is depressing."

"Yeah?"

"*Yeah.* Quasimodo is in love with Esmeralda, and it's completely hopeless. And before this, we read *The Grapes of Wrath.* You can't tell me you didn't want to give up and die after that one. Just once I'd like to read a book with a happy ending. But it won't be anytime soon. She's having us read *The Scarlet Letter* next."

"We're reading short stories now."

"Slacker," Addie said, pushing her chair back from the computer. "Do you want anything to eat?"

I wanted her to be in a better mood when I asked her to the dance, so I decided to wait for a few minutes. "Sure."

"Let's see what we've got." We ended up at the kitchen table watching the Shermans' popcorn popper spit kernels out into a bowl.

It was loud, and I decided not to yell out, "Do you want to go to the Valentine's Day dance with me?" over the noise. Asking someone out in person is fine, but yelling at her while you do it isn't.

But when the last kernel had popped, Addie started talking before I had a chance. "So have you heard if Rob's going to the Valentine's dance or not?"

"He's going."

"Huh." Addie was quiet for a second. "He's probably taking Brook, right?"

"I think so." This was as good a chance as any. She'd given me an opening.

Still, I didn't say anything. The expression on her face made me stop. She looked a little sad. What was going on?

It only took a second before I got it. Addie liked Rob.

I probably could have figured that one out a long time ago if I'd been paying attention. It all started to make sense. I remembered that weird conversation we'd had back in December before the Holiday Formal. It should have been obvious to me then.

Once I had that big revelation, I knew I wasn't going to ask her to the dance anymore. I wouldn't want to go just to watch her watching Rob and Brook all night. *She* wouldn't want to go with me and have to watch Rob and Brook all night. We could save ourselves a lot of trouble and go snowboarding with Cody instead, if her parents would let her.

No wonder it had been so hard for Addie when Brook had started coming with us on Fridays. She'd had to see the person she liked flirt with someone else. And she'd had to try to pretend she didn't feel anything except friendship for him. I knew just how she felt.

CHAPTER 9

FEBRUARY

Caterina Giovanni

Neither Jenna nor I mentioned the guy in our room after that night. She was all friendly again the next day, so I decided not to tell Noelle and Liz.

I know avoiding things isn't the best policy, but I didn't want to ruin everything right when the four of us were starting to hang out more as a group. After a few days had passed, I felt like I'd made the right choice. Jenna was hanging out with us more, and I hadn't seen the guy again. I convinced myself that it had been a one-time thing.

"Cate, your cell phone's ringing," Jenna called from our room. "Do you want me to answer it?"

"No, I've got it."

She met me at the door with my phone in her hand. "Who's Steve?" she asked, glancing at the display.

"A friend." I took the phone from her and turned away as I answered the call. "Hey!"

"Hey, what are you up to?" he asked me.

"Not much. We had an intramural volleyball game the other day."

"Did you win?"

"Of course," I said indignantly. "What do you take me for?"

"You're right. I should have known."

"What about you? What are you doing?"

"I'm standing by the mailbox waiting for the mailman. I got bored, so I thought I'd call you. I'm freezing."

"You're waiting for your mission call, aren't you?"

"Yup. It should be here any day now."

"Go inside and wait. You can watch through the window. You're not wearing a coat, are you?"

"Nope." Steve hates wearing a coat, even when it's frigid outside.

"Seriously, Steve. Go inside."

"All right," he said, and I could hear the sound of snow crunching under his feet. "I'm going in, but I'm not leaving the window until I see the mailman."

"Wasn't it about this time last year that you were stalking the mailman in Ithaca?" The year before, Steve had had a hard time deciding between BYU and Binghamton for college. He'd put his acceptance letter to BYU into the mailbox, only to change his mind right after. So Steve ended up standing by the mailbox until the mailman came. When he did, Steve asked for the letter back so that he could tear it up; he'd sent an acceptance letter to Binghamton instead.

"Oh, yeah. Good thing this is a different mailman or he'd think I was crazy."

"You *are* crazy."

"I know." I heard a door close. "Okay, I'm inside now. I think I need some hot chocolate."

"Good luck. You'd better call me when it comes."

"I will. Talk to you soon."

"Bye." I hung up the phone, smiling at the mental image of Steve smashing his face up against the window like a little kid. The mailman was probably praying that Steve's call would come soon so he wouldn't have Steve lying in wait for him every day.

Noelle and Liz both asked at the same time, "Was that Steve?"

I nodded.

The two gave each other meaningful looks. They were both positive I had this thing for Steve. Lately, I didn't *think* I did. I liked him a lot. He was cute. But we hadn't lived near each other for a year, he was leaving on a mission in a few months, and I knew every single one of his faults. Worse, he knew about mine. I've got a few of them. Shocking, I know.

Also, even though I'm a practical person, I figure I'm entitled to get swept off my feet and fall crazy in love at first sight. That never happened with Steve, and I wanted to keep my options open. You know, in case it happened with someone else.

Noelle and Liz were talking about what we should make for Sunday dinner, the one meal we all ate together every week. Somewhere around the time they were arguing over what to have for dessert, I let my mind wander.

Being nineteen, and a girl, and watching all these nineteen-year-old boys get called on missions is strange. I remembered this guy from our ward who got his call to Russia, and I wondered how that was going to work out. I kept thinking, *I know that guy. I sat by him in Sunday School all last semester. He was always joking around and trying to get the lesson off track. He's never even read the Book of Mormon all the way through, and now he's going to be teaching the gospel—in Russian?*

Of course, Steve is more prepared than that guy. But still. Steve had slept through seminary the first part of his senior year. I practically had to force him to do his job as co-president of our class. Now he was going to be out there trying to motivate people and teach them about the gospel.

Well, I guess we'd *all* be in trouble if we couldn't change.

"Cate. Cate. What do you think?" Noelle shoved the shopping list toward me.

"About what? I wasn't listening."

"I know you weren't. How does this dinner sound for Sunday?"

I scanned the menu. "Looks good. Are you guys going shopping now?"

"Yeah. You're coming, right?"

"Definitely." I didn't have a car, so I always went shopping when Noelle and Liz did. "Is Jenna coming?" She didn't have a car either.

"I'll go ask her." Liz went to the back and knocked on the door. We heard Jenna call, "Come in."

"Jenna, we're all going to the grocery store. Do you want a ride?"

"I'd love one. I'm out of almost everything." Jenna followed Liz out of the room.

By the way, we won the ward lip-sync. Noelle was convinced it was her dance moves. Liz was convinced it was her knowledge of every single word in the song, even the hard part when the chorus got really fast. I told them the reason we'd won was my ability to blend both into a fusion of music and dance that was unparalleled in Rexburg history. They told me I'd been spending too much time at the library and my vocabulary was showing. Jenna laughed at all of us. She hadn't done the dance with us, but she had come along to the activity and flirted with Brett the whole time, which had made me glad. He seemed a lot nicer than the guy who had been in our room.

• • •

"Should we all use the same cart?" Liz asked.

"I'll take my own." Jenna yanked one out from the tangle of metal at the front of the store. "I have a lot of groceries to get."

"Me too." I pulled out a cart.

"I'll share with you," Noelle told Liz. The four of us started walking toward the cereal aisle, which was always our first stop.

Because Liz, Noelle, and I were on an intramural volleyball team together, we were trying to eat healthy. I put a box of Wheaties into my cart. So did Liz. But Noelle reached right past us and pulled down the Apple Jacks. That was our undoing. I put the Wheaties back and picked up some Honey Smacks. Liz traded hers for Lucky Charms.

Jenna was watching us and smiling.

"What's the point of going to college if you can't buy the type of cereal you want, anyway?" I asked.

"I never eat my crusts anymore," Liz announced.

"We're such a bunch of rebels," Noelle said.

Jenna added a box of chocolate cereal to her cart. "I like the prizes," she joked, and we all laughed.

We went up and down the aisles together. It felt like last semester when our old roommate Carrie would go shopping with us. Things were working out.

Noelle and Liz were still looking in the produce when I wheeled my cart over to the refrigerated section for some milk. Jenna was already there. She was putting something into her cart.

It was a six-pack of bottles, labeled Bacardi Silver. She was buying alcohol.

I couldn't believe it.

It didn't make sense, her coming to the grocery store with us and buying alcohol when it was explicitly against the Honor Code and her personal religion. Not to mention against the *law*. Maybe I was wrong. Maybe it wasn't Bacardi Silver. Maybe it was some kind of drink that only looked like Bacardi Silver. And had the same name. And was in the alcoholic beverage section.

I stared too long, and Jenna caught me. Our eyes locked, and she turned away. How was she expecting to get away with *this*?

Neither Noelle nor Liz had seen anything. "We're done," Noelle called. "Are you guys ready?"

"I am," I said, and Jenna echoed me. The four of us headed for the checkout line. I noticed Jenna had tucked her latest selection out of sight, under her bread and packages of Rice-A-Roni and other innocent college staples. I started pushing my cart faster, wanting to buy my food and get out of there. I wanted to put some distance between Jenna and me, so I wouldn't be around when she got busted for being an idiot.

I didn't expect Jenna to follow me into the checkout lane I'd chosen, but she did. She was right behind me. Maybe she figured that since I'd already seen the drinks anyway, it didn't matter. I ignored her while I piled all my stuff onto the belt. Noelle and Liz were buying their groceries a few lanes down, at the counter where the cute guy from Noelle's biology class worked. He and Noelle had an ongoing flirtation from last semester. It was why we all shopped at this particular store.

I wondered if we'd be able to come back after today.

The checkout lady rang me up quickly while I avoided all eye contact with Jenna. I swiped my debit card through the reader, signed the receipt, and headed for the doors, where I stopped and waited for Noelle and Liz. I didn't want to turn around to see what was happening with Jenna, but I couldn't help myself.

I looked back to see her flashing an ID without being asked. The woman looked at it, looked at Jenna, and scanned the Bacardi Silver through. She double-bagged it in a plastic bag so the bottles wouldn't fall out the bottom. Jenna was going to get away with it.

Noelle and Liz joined us. "Guess who just got asked out?" Liz said the minute we were out of the store. "Noelle, that's who."

"He asked me if I wanted to study for the next test with him. That's not the same thing as getting asked out," Noelle said, but she still sounded pleased.

"Well, it's a start." Liz opened the trunk of her car and we all piled our groceries inside. No one noticed Jenna's double-bagged purchase. I didn't bring it up on the drive home because Noelle and Liz couldn't stop talking about Biology Class Boy.

I had to figure out what I was going to say.

• • •

We unloaded the groceries in the kitchen together, except for the contents of one bag, which Jenna disappeared with into our room. Was she drinking it already? I didn't want to find out.

When I finished putting everything on the shelves or in the fridge, I went straight back to our room. Jenna turned to look at me when I opened the door. She was smiling the smile of someone who's trying to be convincing.

"Hey, about that stuff. I'm using it on my hair," she explained. "Don't tell Noelle or Liz. They'll freak out. You've heard of that, right? Washing your hair in beer or wine to give it more body?"

I gave her a look that said, *I don't believe you.* No one goes to all the trouble of getting a fake ID because they're obsessed with washing their hair in expensive alcoholic beverages. How naïve did Jenna think I was? I mean, *come on.* I'd seen stuff this before, and worse. Kids in my high school had fake IDs, exactly like she did. They snuck away on Slope Day at Cornell to get drunk with the college students. I'd driven friends home more than once when a party had gotten out of hand and they'd called me for a ride. But I didn't expect to be dealing with this at a church school. I guess I *was* a little naïve.

"You don't have to believe me," she said, reading my look correctly. "It's none of your business anyway. What are you going to do, tell the bishop?"

I ignored the question. "Actually, you're wrong. It *is* my business. It's in my room. Even if you *were* using it for your hair, you can't keep that in our apartment. We could get in trouble—all of us. So you'd better figure out how you're going to get rid of it. Now."

Jenna picked up the bag. "Wow. Okay, you're really overreacting about this. I'll throw it in the trash."

Before she left, I blocked the door. "And that was lame. Putting it in Liz's car. She would have been the one in trouble if you'd gotten caught."

"I said I won't do it again. I won't go anywhere with you guys again. Are you happy?"

"Not really." The two of us glared at each other. She backed down first and looked away. Or had *I* been the one who backed down first, when I hadn't said anything in the store?

I'd been around plenty of people who had standards different from mine. But this was weird. I'd never been around someone who was supposed to know better and who went ahead and did it anyway. It bugged me way more than it had when my high school friends were being stupid, or when I heard about the things they did on the weekend. They weren't Mormon, after all. Steve might not have been particularly motivated, but he didn't go out of his way to do things he wasn't supposed to do, at least not in front of me.

It wasn't until later that I realized something. Why would she come with us? Why wouldn't she just walk to a gas station or go to the store alone? Why would she follow me into the same checkout lane? Even her lame excuse was one she knew I'd never believe.

She'd *wanted* me to know.

CHAPTER 10

FEBRUARY

Addie Sherman

One summer evening, when I was about nine years old, my whole family went miniature golfing for family night. My brothers kept teasing me about how bad I was. They weren't trying to be mean—they were being brothers—but I kept getting madder as the night went on. I was used to them teasing me, and I had gotten good at ignoring them. But that night, they were driving me crazy. It was hot and sticky, and I was sick of them.

On the last hole, you could win a free round of miniature golf if you got a hole-in-one. It was hard, of course—you had to hit the ball up a ramp, over a small gap, and into a clown's gaping mouth that opened and closed. All my brothers missed, one right after the other. Then it was my turn.

I set my jaw. I knew I would probably miss, and they would tease me. I hit the ball straight and hard. It shot right into the open clown mouth. Bells rang, and flashing lights came on. The clown snapped his mouth shut, and it stayed that way. People started cheering. "Did you see that?" someone asked nearby. "That little girl just got a hole-in-one."

At first, my brothers couldn't believe it. Then they were proud of me. When the manager of the golf course gave me my certificate for a free round, they all wanted to see it and gave me fives, one after the other.

"Do you want to save the game for later or play it now?" my mom asked me. "We can do whatever you'd like."

"I think I'd like to play it now," I told my mom.

So we all played another round, and this time my brothers didn't give me such a hard time. They still teased me, of course, but it was different. They called me Tiger, like Tiger Woods, and they didn't ridicule my golf stance anymore.

That night I learned that even if things are going badly, they might change suddenly. It doesn't happen very often, so I don't count on it, but I learned that when it happens you'd better enjoy it while you can.

So that is exactly what I did when things changed for the better one Friday in February.

. . .

It all started after school when I went to meet up with Rob and Sam, and I overheard the end of what Rob was saying. "Brook isn't coming today. She's got a recital tonight."

He'd barely finished the sentence before Cody joined them. "Rob, my board's still at home. We can get it on the way, right?"

While the two of them were talking, Sam caught my eye. Silently, he held up Rob's car keys, and, with an aura of I'm-up-to-something, he tilted his head toward the hallway that led to the parking lot.

Trying not to draw attention to myself, I pulled on my backpack and moved in his direction. We started walking. Cody and Rob were still talking. We were halfway down the hall when we heard Rob yell, "They've got my keys! Sam! Addie! You *punks!* Do *not* leave without me!"

We sprinted outside. I was laughing hysterically as we each threw open a door and climbed into Rob's car. "Go! Go!" I said, slamming the passenger door shut.

"We don't even have your board," Sam said, laughing and turning to look at me.

"It doesn't matter. Just get us out of here."

"Rob will kill me." Sam pulled out anyway.

"Where are we going?" I asked. Sam's cell phone started ringing. He pulled it out of his pocket and handed it to me.

I looked at the number on the screen. "It's Rob."

"You'd better answer it," Sam said, grinning.

"Hello, you've reached Sam's cell phone. He can't talk right now. He's busy driving a stolen car."

"You two better get back here right now, or you're going to be walking to Snoqualmie Pass." Rob didn't sound too mad.

"He says we'd better get back there now, or he'll start crying," I reported.

"Tell him we're just driving over to your car to load up your board," Sam said loudly. "Tell him not to cry. Tell him we won't abandon him because we need his car too much."

"Did you hear that?" I asked Rob.

"Yeah, I did. Tell Sam that while you guys are driving around, you might as well put some gas in the car."

"Okay." I turned to Sam. "He says we should fill up the car before we go back."

"Anything else?" Sam yelled.

"Actually, yes," said Rob. "I want some jerky, some chips, those chocolate cupcakes with the cream in the middle"—I *knew* he was the guy for me—"Skittles, a corndog, a Hershey's bar—but not the lame kind with only chocolate, I want the kind with the almonds—one of those green air-fresheners that look like Christmas trees—"

"This is getting expensive," I told Sam after I hung up on Rob while he was still listing junk food items and convenience store treasures. "Now he wants us to buy him snacks."

Sam rolled his eyes and headed for the nearest gas station. "Some getaway we're making. Rob's going to beg us to steal his car every week after this."

"We're too responsible to be thieves. We shouldn't have answered the phone. We should have just driven off somewhere alone."

Sam looked over at me, surprised. Oops. *That* hadn't come out sounding the way I'd meant it to. Luckily, we'd pulled up next to the gas pump, and I hopped out to hide my embarrassment. Sam followed me.

"I'll take care of this," I said, unscrewing the gas cap. "You go get the snacks. I never know what kind of junk you guys are going to want."

"Oh, right, Miss Jerky-Is-So-Stinky-But-I'll-Eat-Ten-Sticks." Sam grabbed the gas pump. "*You* get the food. Then you won't be able to complain the whole way up."

"Fine." I tossed the gas cap at him. He didn't catch it fast enough and it bounced off his arm, rolling under the car. "But you better like what I pick out."

"Okay, okay. I won't complain." He shook his head at me.

I hurried through the convenience store, grabbing plenty of Hostess cupcakes and a big bottle of the flavor of Gatorade Sam liked best. I also got granola bars (which the guys would make fun of, but then eat anyway) and jerky, of course. And wintergreen gum. On my way to the counter, I grabbed a pine-scented air freshener, too, smiling to myself.

Sam came in while I was at the register. "What is this?" he asked, picking up the gum. "*Minty* gum? Guys don't chew minty gum. We chew cinnamon gum."

I handed the cashier my money. "You're chewing minty gum today, and you're gonna like it."

He made a face at me. Then he held up the air freshener. "What's this?"

I started blushing. "It's a joke—Rob said he wanted one. He was kidding, but I thought it would be funny to get him one . . ."

Sam handed it back. He had a strange look on his face, like he was going to say something, but he didn't. We walked back to the car in an awkward silence. Sam started the car and pulled away from the pump.

"Did you remember to pick up the gas cap?" I asked him, suddenly remembering.

He slammed on the brakes and shifted into reverse, driving back to the pump. He jumped out. I rolled down the window and stuck my head out to ask if he'd found the cap.

He had. It flew in the window right next to my head.

"*Sam!* That almost hit me!"

He ran around the front of the car and climbed back into the front seat. "I know. But it didn't, because I have great aim."

"Liar. You have terrible aim. You were trying to hit me in the head and you missed."

"Wrong. My aim is *perfect,* Sherman. I was aiming for the cupholder, and I made it." I turned around. The gas cap was perched in the cupholder. Sam grinned at me, grabbed the cap, and went around to put it back on the car. When he climbed back in, he seemed to have forgotten all about the air freshener.

· · ·

Half an hour later, riding shotgun, eating jerky, joking with Rob and Sam and Cody, pretending Brook didn't exist, and watching the little green tree swing back and forth on the rearview mirror, I suddenly realized something very important.

"Pull over," I said to Rob. "I think I'm going to be sick."

He laughed. "Come on. The music isn't that bad."

"No, Rob, I'm serious. I think it's the air freshener. Or the jerky. Or both."

Sam leaned up between the front seats to look at me. "Rob, she's not kidding. Pull over."

I hopped out and crashed through the snowdrifts at the side of the road, waving off Sam's call of, "Are you okay?" I made it far enough away that hopefully Rob didn't see me lose my lunch (and everything else I'd eaten afterward) in the snow. I stood there for a second, making sure I was okay. I felt normal again, but I realized I would have to ask Rob to get rid of the air freshener. I bet Brook never threw up on their dates. I complained about Sam and Rob and Cody treating me like one of the guys, but I wasn't being very dainty today.

Mortified, I climbed back into the car. No one said a word for what seemed like a very long minute or two, and then: "I have some minty gum," Sam offered, handing me the pack.

• • •

Cody had to go inside the lodge for awhile because of too much jerky, and none of the rest of us wanted to ride up alone. So we broke our usual rule and smashed all three of us onto the same lift chair over on Blackhawk. Both Sam and Rob made plenty of unnecessary comments about how grateful they were I had picked up some gum, and they started to make up commercials about it on the lift.

"Rob, I can't believe how *fresh* my mouth feels!" Sam said.

"Me either!" Rob chewed his gum loudly. "It's like a forest of candy canes . . . in my mouth!"

"Me too!" Sam said. "It's like a mint party . . . *in my mouth!*"

"It's like I could throw up and then chew this gum, and it wouldn't even matter!"

"Stop it, you guys," I said, laughing uncontrollably.

"Remember when you used to be so quiet around us, Addie?"

Rob asked. "Remember the first time we all went boarding, and you sat in the back and didn't say a word? Cody decided you hated him."

"I do," I joked.

"No, seriously, what happened? Now we can't get you to stop talking."

"And you always eat all our jerky."

"And you're so comfortable around us that you'll even throw up and then breathe all over us like nothing happened."

Maybe it wasn't so bad to be one of the guys. I sat on the lift with the wind in my hair while they laughed and joked, and I wished things would never change, too happy to remember that they already had.

CHAPTER 11

FEBRUARY

Sam Choi

Stupid Alex, with his stupid comment about Mom and her paint samples. The Saturday before Mikey's wedding, she accosted us at breakfast. She plunked down three big cans of paint on the kitchen table and smiled.

"I'm finally going to take you two up on your Christmas gift. I need you to paint the living room today. I want to do it before the wedding, and if we paint today, the smell should be gone in time."

"Mom, we're not even having the reception here," I protested.

"I know, but people will be coming in and out, and I want the house to look nice. I'm going to help, and so is your dad."

Not only does Dad hate painting, he also has a bad back. He wouldn't be helping much, but at least we'd all be in it together.

"It's going to look great," Mom told me, popping open one of the paint cans to show me the color. It looked like mashed peas. When she saw my face, she added, "It's sage green. You'll love it when it's up on the walls."

Love seemed like a strong word to use for paint the color of baby food.

• • •

Painting was slow going. Mom had specific ideas about the way things should be done. She didn't trust either of us to do the trim or around the windows, so Alex and I were supposed to do the "easy" part with the big paint rollers.

Still, Alex was not living up to her standards.

"Alex! Use smaller strokes!"

"No, Alex, don't leave white spots. You have to make sure they're covered before you move on to another part of the wall."

Finally, Alex put down his roller in exasperation. "I'm going to get some food. I'm starving."

"I'll go with you," said Dad. I could tell his back was killing him.

"Bring us all some lunch, all right?" Mom asked. "I bet Sam and I could use a break by the time you get back."

Actually, Sam could use a break right now. "Just a minute." I set my roller back in its puddle of sage-green paint.

A look of panic crossed Mom's face.

"Don't worry, I'll be right back," I promised. "I'm gonna make a phone call. It'll be quick. I'm going to see if Addie will come over and help." I'd been thinking about who I could call to make this job go faster: Cody, Rob, Addie . . . Addie was most likely to say yes, and the only one capable of living up to Mom's high standards. Cody wouldn't last a second.

Plus, Addie and I had been each other's go-to person for years. So what if she liked Rob? She didn't know that I knew. We could still be friends. I was over it.

As I dialed her number, I heard Alex and Dad congratulating each other on their escape. Losers.

Addie answered the phone.

"Hey, I have a favor to ask," I said.

"What is it?"

"We're painting the living room right now, and I was wondering if you would mind helping for awhile. I'm going crazy."

"Let me check with my mom. I've spent all morning working on homework, so I bet she'll say it's okay. I'll call you back if it isn't."

I went back to painting, but I kept looking through the living room window to see if she'd arrived. It wasn't long before I saw a car pull up near the curb. Addie jumped out, waved to her mom, and then jogged up the sidewalk. Her brother Dave was a cross-country runner, and Addie would have been a good one too, but she hated organized sports. I opened the door right as she was about to knock.

"Hey."

"Hey."

"Thanks for coming. It's only me and Mom now. I think Alex managed to get himself fired."

"But you didn't?"

"I'm too competent." As we headed toward the living room, I decided to warn her. "Don't mention the color. It's looking weird, but I don't want to repaint this."

"Okay."

"This is so sweet of you," Mom said to Addie. "I don't know how Sam and I ended up doing this whole thing ourselves."

"I do," I muttered under my breath.

I kept using the big roller while Mom and Addie painted near the trim. I was hoping the color would get lighter as it dried. It did, but not by much. I caught Addie's eye as she dipped her brush in the paint and made a face. I started to smile, and she looked away. Luckily, Mom didn't notice. She was still happy with the paint color, and, like I'd told Addie, I wanted to keep it that way.

. . .

A little while later, Alex and Dad arrived with the burgers.

"Finally!" I put my roller back in the tray. "I'm starving. Come eat." Addie set her brush down on the plastic and stood up, stretching.

Mom bustled into the kitchen ahead of us to pull out plates and glasses. I took my chance. "So what do you think?" I asked Addie in a low voice. "Is it looking as bad as I think it is?"

Addie tried not to laugh. "It's . . . different."

"It looks like we're in a Dr. Seuss book."

This time she did laugh. "It's not *that* bad. It could be worse. A lot worse."

"You're right. Things can always be worse."

We didn't talk much as we painted in the afternoon. The sunlight came angling through the window, turning parts of the walls different shades of green.

"So what's the real color?" I asked Mom. "The color that it is when the sunlight is on it, or the color it is when it's dark and the inside lights are on?"

"That sounds like one of those philosophical questions, like the one about the tree falling in the woods."

"That means you don't know the answer."

She dabbed a little more paint in a spot near the window. "What do you think, Addie?"

"Oh, I don't know. It could just be whatever one you like the best."

"Wow, Ad, that was profound," I teased her.

"Don't make me throw this paintbrush at you," she warned, and then hurried to reassure my mom. "Don't worry, Mrs. Choi, I'm kidding. I promise."

• • •

After we'd finished, it was late in the afternoon. I had remembered while we were painting that it was Addie's birthday sometime this month, and I thought we should celebrate. Maybe if it weren't for a few days, Rob and Cody and I could come up with a plan.

"Hey, your birthday is coming up, right?"

"It's tomorrow."

Dang. I was just in time. "I was thinking we should do something about that. Do you want to go to dinner and see a movie tonight? Or does your family have big plans for you already?"

"Not for tonight. I'd like that. What do you want to see?"

"Whatever you want. It's your birthday."

Addie pretended to think for a minute. "How about that one with the girl who is in love with a guy, but then he dies, so she has to try to find a way to communicate with him, but meanwhile, she's falling in love with his best friend . . ." She trailed off and burst out laughing when she looked at the expression on my face. "Don't worry, I was only kidding."

I tried to act chivalrous. "We can go to that one if that's the one you want to see."

"No, no, no. I don't want to see it either."

I went into the kitchen to arrange for transportation for the night. Mom was rinsing her paintbrush in the sink, so I decided to ask her instead of Dad. Her car was nicer anyway.

"Hey, Mom, Addie and I are going to get some dinner and see a movie. Is it all right if I use your car?"

"You're taking Addie on a *date?*" Alex asked loudly.

I ignored him. "Can I use the car?"

"Of course," Mom said, beaming. She came out to say good-bye and to thank Addie one more time for all her help.

I'd wanted to hang out with Addie for her birthday, but for some reason I hadn't realized how much like a . . . well, like a *date* the movie would be. Dinner was normal—we ate and talked and laughed—but the movie was different. I didn't think about it until the lights went down in the theater, and I suddenly felt awkward. I wasn't trying to put the moves on her or anything, but I was worried she might think I was. I didn't want to freak her out or make things weird. I knew she didn't like me. She liked Rob.

Still, the whole time I was thinking how cool it would have been if she *had* liked me. Then I could have reached over and held her hand, or leaned in as close as I wanted to whisper in her ear.

Anyway. The movie wasn't bad, and Addie is one of those people who only makes comments when absolutely necessary, which I appreciate. I hate it when people talk through the whole movie. Also, she's always saying she isn't funny like her older brothers, but she cracks me up when she makes her little comments about the movie, or about life in general. She is funny. She doesn't give herself enough credit sometimes.

• • •

I drove Addie home after the movie because I was supposed to get back and help with some wedding-related project. I couldn't remember what, but I knew there was something. There was always something.

Bubbles. That was it. I was supposed to help Mom tie red ribbons around all these little containers of bubbles that the guests were going to blow when Mikey and Ethan left after the reception. Mom said it would be less messy than throwing rice and more beautiful. I thought it was a good call on her part. Alex and I could have done some serious damage if we'd been allowed to throw rice.

Who comes up with this stuff anyway? *Bubbles? Rice?* Spending your Saturday night tying little red ribbons around hundreds of tiny containers?

"What do you think is going on with Rob and Brook?" Addie asked me as we pulled into her driveway.

"What do you mean, what's going on?"

"I mean, do you think they're together?"

"Isn't it obvious?" I didn't want to hurt her feelings, but it *was* pretty obvious.

"Well, yeah, but do you think it's serious? She hasn't been sixteen for very long. And Rob's graduating this year."

"I don't know. It seems like they're serious. They're together all the time." Then like an idiot, I blurted out, "What do you care?"

Addie was silent. Her face was bright red.

"You like Rob, don't you." There, I'd said it. I don't know why I was trying to make her say the actual words. I already knew.

I guess I wasn't as cool with the whole thing as I'd thought.

Addie was turning even redder. "Don't tell him. I feel stupid."

"Why would you feel stupid? Lots of girls like Rob."

"That's exactly why I feel stupid," Addie said. "I don't want him to know I'm one of those dumb girls with a crush on him. Then everything would be all weird."

I was worried I'd ruined the whole night. She looked so embarrassed. "I promise not to say anything."

"You don't think he already knows, do you?"

I was still trying to fix things. "No, I bet he doesn't. You're just like one of the guys, anyway."

"Thanks a lot." Addie turned to glare at me. If she hadn't looked so mad, I would have sworn she was crying. Her eyes seemed kind of teary.

"What? I didn't mean that in a bad way."

"Sure you didn't." She opened the car door.

"Addie, I'm sorry," I said before she slammed the door. I opened my door and called out to her again as she walked up the sidewalk. "I'm sorry!"

She kept going.

CHAPTER 12

FEBRUARY

Caterina Giovanni

Noelle was the star of our intramural game. Biology Class Boy (whose real name was actually Noah) had come to watch. Noelle had been in top form, scoring five of our points. Liz and I teased her that love brought out the best in her game. Liz and I weren't too shabby ourselves. We annihilated the other team.

I love winning.

My cell phone rang right as we were climbing into Liz's car to go get shakes and celebrate. It was Steve. He barely waited for me to say hello before he started talking. "Cate! I got it!"

"Your mission call?"

"What else? You want to know where I'm going?"

"Of course I do!"

"You have to guess."

"All right. Um . . . Russia?"

"Nope." Then he just blurted it out. Steve has never been very good at keeping the suspense going. "I'm going to Munich, Germany."

"That's great! Congratulations!"

"Thanks. I'm supposed to leave at the end of June. You'll be back by then, right?"

"Definitely. Even if I get that job in Seattle, I'll be back by mid-June. We should be able to hang out before you go."

"Awesome. Hey, do you have Andrea and Joel's phone number? I want to give them a call too."

"I've got it right here." I gave him the number.

"Thanks. Okay, I have to call some other people. You're the first one I called outside of my family."

"Really?" I was flattered.

"Well, you helped me get here. Hey, I'll call you again soon. I want to hear about what you're doing." I could hear people in the background. "That's my family. I better go."

"All right. Congratulations again. Talk to you soon." I hung up.

"So . . ." Liz drawled. "Where's he going?"

"Munich, Germany. He leaves in June."

They both grinned at me.

"What?" I said.

"You know you like him," Liz said.

"I don't know how *you* can know that, since *I* don't know that myself."

"Fine. We *think* that because you get all defensive and weird whenever we ask about him," Noelle said. "Like you're getting right now. Plus, Andrea told me that you and Steve were practically inseparable at the end of last year."

"She did?" I was going to have to talk to Andrea about giving her cousin too much information.

"And we've seen pictures of him. He's hot," Liz added.

"Super hot," said Noelle.

"Hotter than Biology Class Boy," I agreed.

Noelle pretended to be mad at me the rest of the way to the drive-thru.

• • •

94

When we walked into the apartment, we could hear a grating, hacking sound coming from the back, near the bathroom I shared with Jenna.

"What is *that?*" Noelle asked.

"It sounds like someone throwing up," I said, going into the back to check. The bathroom door was closed, but I knocked and then pushed it open slowly. Jenna was curled up on the floor. She looked up at me but had to turn back to the toilet before either of us could say anything. I could tell by the smell and by the zoned-out look on her face that she was drunk.

I went back to Noelle and Liz. "It's Jenna. She's sick. She's throwing up." That was all I said. For some reason, I was still keeping Jenna's secrets for her. I didn't know exactly why. I was closer to the other two girls than I was to Jenna, but I kept covering for her and trying to smooth everything over.

I guess I felt responsible. She was my roommate, although I hadn't chosen her. I wanted to give her the benefit of the doubt. Besides, every time she did something wrong and I called her on it, she didn't do it again. She'd thrown the alcohol away, and I hadn't seen her drink any of them. There hadn't been any more guy-in-our-room incidents.

Still, the situation was weird. I didn't have any shared history with Jenna. We didn't have a long friendship we could draw on or past experiences we could laugh about together. I had no idea what her family was like, or what her life was like, or even what *she* was like. Though, once in awhile, I caught a glimpse of someone fun and interesting. All I had to work with was a couple of months living in the same room and a feeling that she was someone who needed help. I wasn't sure how to get it for her, though.

"Uh-oh," Noelle said. "Does she need to go to the doctor?"

"I don't know. We'll have to see if she gets worse."

Jenna was lying on her bed when I went back into the room. She rolled over and pretended to sleep. I let her. But I knew I couldn't let much more time pass without talking about things. I knew her alarm would go off first thing the next morning, the way it always did. And, this time, I knew I would be waiting. Something had to change.

. . .

I was awake long before Jenna's alarm went off. I sat bolt upright when it started beeping, a shrill and demanding sound in the still of the morning, and I quietly moved toward the wall. When she hit snooze, I flipped the light switch and flooded the room with brightness. She rolled over and looked at me. I stood next to her bed with my arms folded. Sometime during the night, my pity had turned into frustration. It wasn't the best feeling to have for the conversation that needed to take place.

"We have to talk," I told her. "You can't keep doing this."

"Doing what? Sleeping in?"

"You know what I'm talking about. Drinking, breaking the rules."

"Why not?"

"Because it's not right."

She was angry. "So you're telling me what to do. You think you know all about me."

"I don't know anything about you. But I can tell that something is up."

"Nothing's up. This is the way I've been for a long time."

"Then why would you come to BYU–Idaho?"

"Because my parents wanted me to."

"Do your parents also want you to go on probation or get expelled? Because that's what's going to happen."

"Are you threatening to turn me in?"

"No, I'm not." I saw her relax a little. "I'm not *threatening* you, Jenna. I'm telling you that you have to talk to someone about this." She tensed up again. "I was hoping *you* would decide to take care of it. You could tell your parents, or talk to the bishop."

She shook her head. "That's not going to happen."

"Why not?"

"It's just not. If you're so worried about it, go ahead and tell someone." She stood up and started getting ready for class. Neither of us said another word. We both knew what was happening.

She was calling my bluff, assuming I was too weak to do anything about it, because that's how I'd been so far.

• • •

It was time to talk to my roommates. And then it would be time to talk to someone else. But who? Her parents, the bishop, the Honor Code office? It all seemed like tattling.

College is a raw deal. How did I end up being responsible for this person who was basically a stranger? I wasn't responsible, was I? Couldn't someone else take care of it?

I couldn't shake the feeling of accountability. Yeah, Jenna kept making mistakes. No, I didn't know her very well. But she was a person who was struggling, and I couldn't keep pretending that nothing was happening.

• • •

I hadn't had a chance to talk to Noelle or Liz yet when Jenna got home that evening. The three of us had been busy all day deciding where we wanted to live the next year, checking out apartments and getting housing contracts from the complexes we liked best. We had been in and out of places all day, and there had almost always been someone else around.

Jenna was in a friendly mood, probably to make up for the night before. "What are you guys doing?" she asked us, sitting down at the table.

"We're signing our housing contracts for next year," Noelle said.

There was an uncomfortable pause. We hadn't invited Jenna to go apartment hunting with us. It hadn't been intentional on Noelle and Liz's part. We'd decided to start looking on the spur of the moment when we all ended up home for lunch and realized we had a free afternoon.

On my part, it might have been somewhat intentional. I honestly didn't want to live with her again next year, not with all the craziness going on.

"Do you guys have a fourth person? I'm still looking around. If you need someone else, I could sign up with you," Jenna offered.

"Why not? I think I grabbed an extra application." Liz slid it across the table toward Jenna. "It's more expensive than this place, but it's closer to campus."

"Oh, I've been to this complex before," Jenna said, looking at the application. "I like it a lot."

The three of them started talking about deposits and rent and everything. I didn't join in, hoping the conversation would end quickly. I had to talk to Noelle and Liz *now*. I shouldn't have waited so long.

I hadn't thought Jenna would want to live with us next year, not after our confrontation.

Jenna signed her contract, and then she went to her room for her checkbook. She wrote out the deposit check. "Do you guys mind taking this back when you take yours?" she asked. I noticed she deliberately did not hand the application and check to me.

"We can do that," Liz said.

"Are you feeling better?" Noelle asked. "We heard you last night. That sounded rough. Was it the flu?"

"It must have been some twenty-four-hour bug," Jenna said. "I feel better now." She stood up, right when the doorbell rang. "Oh, I think that's my date." She opened the door, and it was Brett.

"I'll see you guys later tonight," she said cheerfully.

"See you," the three of us called back. The door closed behind her, and I turned to look at Liz and Noelle.

"You guys, we have to talk," I said. "We *really* have to talk."

"Whoa, this sounds like a big deal," teased Liz.

"Are you about to admit that you like Steve?" Noelle squealed.

"I'm serious. It has nothing to do with Steve."

They both stopped grinning. "Okay, what is it?" Noelle asked.

"Are you okay?" Liz leaned toward me. "You've been acting out of it all day."

"I'm fine. But Jenna's not."

"She said she's feeling better," Noelle said.

"I know, but she's still not *really* better. She was drunk last night. It wasn't a virus. And there have been a couple of other things too." I told them about the night she'd had the guy in our room after hours, and about the time at the grocery store when she bought the drinks and then hid them on our way out.

It was quiet for a second. Then Noelle spoke.

"Are you *positive?*"

That made me a little mad. "*Yes.* I saw her buy the Bacardi Silver. I saw the guy in my room, and I saw what time it was. And I know what I saw last night!"

"Okay, okay. Stupid question."

"Why didn't you tell us before?" Liz asked me.

"I kept thinking that each thing was a one-time mistake. I kept thinking things were going to get better."

"You should have told us," Liz said firmly. "That was my car she was riding in! I could have been busted!"

"I know. I was wrong." I didn't know what else to say. It was true. So I said it again, "I was wrong. I should have told you both right away. But I kept thinking she wouldn't do anything else."

"So what now?" Noelle asked.

"I don't know," I said. "This is so weird. I've had friends who've done stuff like this before, but none of them were people I actually lived with."

"We could talk to the bishop," Noelle suggested.

"Or her parents," Liz added.

"I think we should have her do it," I said. "I know that hasn't worked yet, but we could tell her we'll give her a couple of days to talk to someone, and if she doesn't, then we'll have to take action. We could tell her that we'll call the Honor Code office."

"Would we do that?" Noelle asked.

Even though it was my suggestion, I was wondering the same thing.

"Yes, we would," Liz said decisively. "It's been more than a month. She's had plenty of chances. We can't let it go on like this."

Noelle sighed. "This is going to be so awkward. I like Jenna."

I agreed. In spite of everything, I kept feeling there was a person behind all of the baggage whom I could like. Maybe that was part of why I felt so responsible for what happened to her.

"No wonder she's been hard to get to know," Liz said. "She has a lot to hide."

"Why do you think she wants to live with us next year?" Noelle asked.

"She might like us. Who knows?" Liz shrugged.

I had a sudden realization. "I wonder if the way I've been acting makes her think she could live with us and get away with everything. She probably thinks I've told you guys and that we're all going to turn the other way."

"Well, if that's it, she won't want to live with us after we talk to her tonight." Noelle sighed. "But we have to do it. We can't pretend it's not happening."

"We can't let her storm off or leave. We have to have it out and talk through it," Liz agreed.

"We've got to be nice about it, though," Noelle said.

"Oh, definitely." Liz paused. "What do we say? This is hard. I wish we knew her better."

"What would make her do all of this? She knows better. Remember when she taught that Relief Society lesson and bore her testimony about the importance of following the commandments and all that? It seems so hypocritical now." I shook my head.

"Mormons can be hypocritical," Liz said. "You know that."

"Well, they shouldn't be."

No one spoke for a few seconds.

"We'll wait until she gets home," Noelle said. "Even if it takes all night."

"Some Friday night this is turning out to be," I observed. "Our roommate is having all the fun for us."

"We should at least watch a movie." Liz started stacking up our standbys—*Pride and Prejudice, Enchanted, Hairspray*—so we could choose.

• • •

Two movies later, the three of us sat in the living room, still waiting. There was a pan of Rice Krispies treats in the middle of the coffee table, and we were all wearing our pajamas. We kept turning toward the door whenever we heard a sound in the hallway. In between our movies, we'd gone over and over what we were going to say. We had different outlines for different scenarios—what we would do if she came home with a guy, what we would do if she came home with Brett, what we would do if she came home as normal as could be. We planned it all out and had our ammunition ready. We were going to be kind, but firm. We were going to be honest. We were going to let her know that we wanted to be her friends, but also that we were united about getting this resolved.

Rice Krispies treats. Pajamas. Movies. Three girls talking. If anyone had dropped by to visit, they would have seen what looked like an average night in the lives of some college freshmen.

Finally, we heard voices. A few minutes later, Jenna came inside and closed the door behimnd her. She was alone.

I suddenly felt sorry for her. Her face had the blinky, tired look of someone who had just walked in from the dark. Her puffy jacket was bulky, making her seem small. I felt like she had walked into an ambush.

"Hey, you guys," she said.

"Jenna, we have to talk to you."

CHAPTER 13

FEBRUARY

Addie Sherman

I take back what I said about Avery being quiet. She was meant to be a Sherman after all. Once she started a big project—a reunion for her friends in the summer—she talked to me all the time:

"Would you hand me that magazine, Addie?"

"Could you bring me the phone so I can call this place?"

"Where would you rather have a reunion for your friends—at someone's house, or at a restaurant, or outside?"

"Outside," I answered automatically.

"But if it's outside, it could always rain," Avery mused. "Even in June."

"Reserve a pavilion at the park. In June, it probably won't rain enough to be unbearable."

"Of course." Avery didn't notice the shortness of my answers. I was trying to do my homework. I was also trying not to think about Sam and how I'd been such a jerk on Saturday. I looked back at the book I was trying to read—the most boring book ever, *The Scarlet Letter*—but I hadn't made it through two sentences before Avery asked, "Can you think of who I'd call to look into that? Would it be Parks and Recreation?"

"I have no idea."

"Hmmm," Avery said. I could hear her flipping the pages of the phone book. Then she started laughing. "There's an advertisement for a company that rents out sumo suits to parties. Wouldn't that be a crazy way to welcome Julie home?"

I nodded but didn't look up. I wasn't trying to be rude, but it wasn't as if I knew any of these people very well. Sure, I'd met most of them, and I knew the Becketts because we were in the same ward. Dave had dated Andrea for awhile, but it wasn't like they were *my* friends. I didn't really even know Julie, the girl who was coming home from her mission, the one Avery was throwing the big reunion party for.

I had other things on my mind. I kept staring at *The Scarlet Letter.* I felt like throwing the book against the wall, or tearing out the pages and offering them to Avery to use for her invitations. This was the kind of book they assigned for Honors or AP English, not regular junior English. What on earth did Mrs. Bryant think she was doing? And there was no way to concentrate with Avery breaking in every five seconds to ask me a question. I looked over at her. She was still going through the phone book.

It was good to see her so excited, though. I'd been coming over to help for a month and a half, and the reunion project was the one thing that had kept her the most interested. I was so desperate for help with English that I was almost ready to ask her for help with a paper topic. But she was always busy with her own work and her reunion planning. So I never did. Sometimes I wondered why I was even there. I definitely wasn't getting any help with English, which was supposedly part of the original bargain.

I guess I *had* done my best to close that door when I told Avery and Dave they weren't allowed to ask about my homework.

"I've decided to send out the invitations as soon as possible," Avery was saying. "That way, everyone has plenty of time to plan.

But I've got to get the location figured out so I can put it on the invitations."

"Do you already know when she's coming home? Some missionaries get extensions."

Avery had already thought of that. "Julie doesn't think it's very likely. Her mission president gave her parents special permission to come and pick her up, so her return date is basically set in stone. We'll have the reunion a week after that. Oh! I found it!" She circled a number in the phone book.

I closed my book and stood up. I wasn't getting anywhere with my homework, and I needed something to do. "Do you want a snack?" I asked Avery. Once her morning sickness was finally gone, she loved it when I "cooked." I could make three things: chocolate chip cookies, oatmeal-chocolate chip cookies, and Jell-O. Avery liked them all. We'd been through the menu a few times.

"Sure."

"What do you feel like?"

She thought for a minute. "I think chocolate chip cookies. No, wait. Jell-O." She paused again. "Too bad you can't put chocolate chips in Jell-O."

"Why not? I can try. But it won't be ready for a couple of hours."

"That's fine," she said, reaching for the phone.

I went into the kitchen and made Jell-O the quick-set way. I dumped in the chocolate chips and shoved the bowl into the fridge. If anyone had seen me, they would have thought I was crazy.

I *was* crazy. I'd yelled at Sam on Saturday and completely overreacted and now things were weird with him. I'd tried to fix things by calling later that night.

"Sorry about yelling at you," I said.

"It's okay. I'm sorry I made you mad."

"Don't worry about it. Let's pretend the whole conversation never happened, okay?"

"All right." Sam sounded relieved. I'd hoped that everything would go back to normal, but it had been awkward between us ever since. I guess I shouldn't storm away from people and expect them to still like me. But at least Sam couldn't accuse me of acting like a guy in *that* situation. I'd been pure girl, and it was purely embarrassing. At least Cody still thought I was normal. Assuming Cody thought about anything.

I went back to the living room to see how Avery was doing.

"Guess what?" she asked.

I opened my mouth to reply, but she beat me to it. "I got the pavilion reserved. We're all set. Now I can make the invitations and send them out, and everyone will have plenty of time to plan ahead."

"That's great." I started to reach for *The Scarlet Letter* again, thinking that Avery would start working on her own homework now that the pavilion question was resolved.

But I was wrong. She meant she was going to put the invitations together right that very second. I had only read a couple of pages when she started talking again.

"Can you hook this up to the printer and print out twenty-five copies of this invitation?" She held her laptop toward me.

"Okay." I closed the book for what I decided would be the final time. I'd tried. I was done.

"Wait, wait," she said as I headed for the desk. "There's some special paper I want you to use. It's right on top of the desk. Will you stick that in the printer?"

"Okay." It was easy to see which paper she meant—the thick robin's-egg blue cardstock.

When the printer had finished, I retrieved the invitations and took them back to Avery. "Do you want me to help you with them?"

"That would be great. I'm bad at stuff like this."

"So am I."

"All we have to do is cut a straight line."

"I don't know if I can guarantee even that," I warned her, and she laughed.

The two of us trimmed down the invitations, and then Avery showed me the other paper she'd picked out as the backing. It was supposed to look like an old map of the world, with green and blue for the water, brown for the countries, and cream for the lettering. "I thought this would be meaningful since she's been across the world, and we're all coming from different places to get together."

"I like it," I said. I did. I don't know much about that kind of thing, but I liked the way the colors looked together, and the font she'd picked wasn't too fussy.

"I've never done any scrapbooking or card making. But the lady at the craft store told Dave that anyone could figure this out. You punch a hole through both sheets of paper and then stick this little fastener through to hold the paper together, and you're all set."

"Okay." I looked at her. "But you should know I hate scrap-booking, Avery."

She sighed. "I know. I do too. But Julie loves it. And she knows that I don't usually do things like this so, when she sees that the invitations are homemade, she'll know how much I cared."

I made a hole in the top of the paper with the hole punch. Unfortunately, it was right in the middle of one of the words. "Oops."

Avery didn't get mad. "That's okay. We can print more if we need to. I had Dave get extra paper in case we made some mistakes."

The next time, I got the hole punched in the right spot. But when I grabbed the little fastener to attach the two papers together, I saw we had a problem. The hole from the hole punch was a little too big. The fastener went right through it. It wasn't going to work.

I looked up at Avery, who had just come to the same realization I had. She looked close to tears, and I started to get nervous. Once or twice that had happened, where she looked like she might fall apart over something minor. It scared the heck out of me because she had never been like that before the whole bed rest thing. The tears seemed to come out of nowhere, and I never knew what to do.

"I should have known I wouldn't be able to figure it out," she muttered.

"We could glue them together," I suggested. "Or staple them."

"It won't look the same." She was still on the verge of tears.

I racked my brain, desperately thinking of a solution. Then I thought of something. I could call Brook. Brook loved things like this. I knew because she had made me a scrapbook page of the group of us snowboarding, which I had taken home and stuffed in my desk drawer since I don't have a scrapbook. But even I could tell she knew what she was doing because it looked so professional. If there was a solution to our invitation problem, Brook would be it.

For a moment, I hesitated. Did I really want to ask Brook for help with something so minor? I looked at Avery's face again and decided that I did. Desperate times call for desperate measures.

"I have a friend we could call," I told Avery.

Avery looked more cheerful immediately. "You do? That would be *great*."

I found Brook's phone number in the stake directory. I was in luck. She answered the phone on the first ring.

"Hey, Brook," I said. "This is Addie."

"Addie!" She sounded cheerful. "What's up?"

"Well, actually, I'm helping my sister-in-law make some invitations and it's not working out. I wondered if you had any advice."

"Okay!" Brook liked to talk in exclamation points.

"Well, we're trying to put these fastener things in the invitations to hold the paper together, and we can't get them to work."

"They're called brads," Avery whispered to me, looking at the box.

"They're called brads," I repeated to Brook, wanting to snicker at myself. *Brads. Or Garys. Or Nates. Some man's name, anyway.*

"Oh, those are easy! All you need is a teeny tiny hole punch. Use that first, and then you can put them together super easy."

"A teeny tiny hole punch," I repeated slowly. I was fairly sure we didn't have anything like that in the house. Avery shook her head at me, and my doubts were confirmed.

"I could bring one over. Where are you? Are you at your house?"

"No, I'm at my brother and sister-in-law's house. It's not too far from where I live, but it's still a long ways for you to drive. Thanks anyway. We can figure it out."

"It's no problem. I could totally bring it over right now. I'm not busy."

If she were over here helping us, she wouldn't be with Rob. Plus, it was nice of her to offer. "Actually, that would be great. If you don't mind."

"I wouldn't mind at all! I'd finally feel like I could pay you back for all the snowboarding help."

I gave her the address, and she said she'd be right there.

"She's coming over," I told Avery, stating the obvious.

"With the teeny tiny hole punch?"

"Yeah." Avery and I both started laughing. I was glad to see that the panic had passed. Avery seemed back to normal.

"That's cool of her," Avery said. "Then we can get these stupid invitations out of the way. I bet you're even more sick of them than I am."

I didn't know what to say about that, so I went and checked on the Jell-O instead. It hadn't set up. It looked disgusting. I could only imagine what Dave was going to say when he got home.

About half an hour later, the doorbell rang, and I went to answer it. Brook was standing there, holding the hole punch, and there was no Rob in sight. "Hi!" she said.

"Thanks for doing this." I held the door open for her to come in.

"It's no big deal," she said, following me into the family room.

Avery was sitting up, and you couldn't tell she'd been close to tears. It seemed like everything had been smoothed right over.

"Brook, this is my sister-in-law, Avery. Avery, this is my friend Brook."

"Thanks for coming over," Avery said. "Did Addie tell you how hopeless we are?" She showed Brook the invitations.

"These are cute!" Brook said. From the look on Avery's face, I didn't think she'd been going for "cute," but she didn't say anything. Brook didn't notice. "It won't take us long to finish them."

She was right. Five minutes later, everything was put together and sealed up in little envelopes.

"Thanks, you guys," Avery said. "Now all I have to do is put addresses on them tonight, and I can send them off."

"No problem," Brook said. I assumed she'd want to get out of there and be on her way, but she just sat on the couch, looking like she planned on staying for awhile. Avery and I looked at each other.

"Would you like anything to eat?" Avery asked. "Addie made us a treat earlier." When she looked at me I could tell she was just remembering that she had changed her order from chocolate chip cookies to chocolate chip Jell-O.

"What are you guys having?"

I paused, feeling stupid. "Really weird Jell-O. It's strawberry, and we put some chocolate chips in it. Actually, it needs an hour or more to set. At least."

"Oh, that's okay. It sounds interesting!"

"So are you a junior at Lakeview too?" Avery asked.

"Oh, I don't go to Lakeview. I go to Eastshore. I know Addie from snowboarding on Fridays. And we're in the same stake."

"Then it was *really* nice of you to drive all the way over here to help us out," Avery said. "I didn't know you were coming from that far away. I'm sure you had better things to do than deliver hole punchers."

"Actually, I was glad Addie called for a couple of reasons. First of all, I owe her a few favors from all the help she's given me."

"And what was the other reason?" Avery asked conversationally.

"I wanted an excuse to rebel."

We were assisting in a rebellion? That I couldn't picture at all. "You did?" I asked.

"I was supposed to be practicing the violin, and I didn't want to." Brook looked at the two of us as if we were going to be shocked by her revelation. I tried not to laugh.

I could see from the look on Avery's face that she didn't think it was much of a rebellion either. "Are you going to get into trouble?" she managed to ask with a straight face.

"No, but my mom won't be thrilled," Brook admitted. "I mean, I'll do it later and everything, but my parents are strict. I'm supposed to practice the violin before I go anywhere, and today I wanted to get out for awhile."

"How long have you been playing the violin?" Avery asked.

"Since I was five."

"Wow."

"She's amazing," I told Avery. "She played at a stake fireside last year, and everyone was impressed."

Brook groaned. "That was so embarrassing! I was so nervous, and I messed up a lot."

"You couldn't tell."

"I don't like performing in front of people I know. I don't mind when it's in a recital hall with a big audience and a judge, but it's harder for me when I know everyone in the audience." She looked at me. "That's why I quit dancing. Do you remember how I would cry before every performance?"

"No. I was too busy throwing a fit. Do you remember how *I* got in trouble for messing up the steps every time?"

Avery was laughing. "You two were in dance class together? Addie, I had no idea! That seems so . . ."

"Out of character?" I finished. "I know. Mom promised me a snowboard if I kept going."

Avery couldn't stop laughing.

"It's not that funny," I told her.

"It's just that I used to be in dance too, and I was the same way," she said.

"No you weren't." There was no way Avery would have ever done ballet.

"I'm serious. Wait. I'll prove it. Go upstairs and get the photo album. It's on top of the dresser in my room."

I couldn't pass this up. Avery had taken ballet? I ran up the stairs and into her room. It was weird going in there, but I found the album as fast as I could and ran back down.

"Here." Avery pointed to a short, skinny girl with long brown hair and a big scowl on her face, sitting in the middle of a row of girls wearing pink, fluffy dancing dresses.

I started laughing. "I have a picture almost exactly like this! Except *I'm* the one sitting there looking ticked off."

"Look closely at that picture when you get home," Brook said to me. "I'm on the very end of the row, bawling my eyes out."

"I never even noticed. I'll have to check it out."

"Too bad none of us stuck with it," Avery joked. "The world has missed out on three prima ballerinas."

"*Right,*" Brook and I said at the same time, and then we all cracked up.

I went into the kitchen to see if the Jell-O was ready yet. It wasn't even close—in fact, it looked like it wasn't going to set up, ever. I showed it to Brook and Avery, and we decided it looked like a science experiment gone horribly wrong.

So Brook and I made chocolate chip cookies and the three of us ate those instead. We traded some more dance class horror stories. Then Brook decided she'd better go home before she got into too much trouble.

"Thanks, you guys! That was fun!"

"Thank *you*," I told her. "You saved the day."

After Brook left, Avery stretched and reached for the last cookie. "I liked her a lot. She's sweet, and I mean that as a compliment."

"Yeah, she is," I agreed.

"It was nice to have someone over. It made the afternoon go faster." Avery looked worried. "No offense."

"Don't worry about it." I wasn't offended. It *had* made things go faster.

In the month or so since I'd started visiting Avery, I'd noticed the amount of visitors had dropped off. The first few times I'd been over, someone had always been coming by to see her, or bring her a gift, or hang out with her. But the traffic had died down as people got preoccupied again with their own lives, and Avery faded into the distance. Maybe that was why she was so edgy, or why she sometimes seemed about to cry. It had to be lonely, hanging out here all day. I knew she missed Dave. They both seemed to live for the moment at the end of the day when he walked in the door, and they were together again.

• • •

When I got home, I went straight to the bookshelves in the family room and pulled out the photo album. There was Brook, bawling at one end of the row. I was sitting at the other end, frowning at the camera. In between us were lots of perfectly poised little girls who liked ballet and who looked right at home. I'd never noticed Brook in that picture before. I'd only been looking at myself.

"Hi, sweetie." My mom came into the room, and I closed the album. "How are Dave and Avery doing?"

"They're hanging in there."

"Did you get your homework finished?"

"I got a start on it." No point in telling her that it was a false start. I still had hopes I could put off telling my parents about my grades until after the snowboarding season was basically over. It was going to be close, but I might be able to do it.

"Remember, you have to keep your grades above a 3.0 if you

want to keep snowboarding so much," my mom said. "That was the deal. You know that."

"I know. I will."

My mom yawned. "Well, I'm heading to bed. I have to be up early again tomorrow."

"Okay." I put the album back on the shelf and turned around. Mom was still standing there.

"Is there anything you want to talk about, hon?"

"Not really. Avery seems to be doing okay, considering everything that's going on."

"I meant anything about *you*."

I shook my head. "I don't think so, Mom."

"All right then." She turned to leave. "Good night, honey."

"See you in the morning," I called after her.

I thought about working on my paper, and I got as far as pulling the book out of my bag before I decided to give up until the next day. I left my things on the kitchen table as proof of my good intentions in case my parents came down during the night or early in the morning.

On my way up the stairs, I heard the sound of lowered voices, and I stopped short before reaching the landing.

"I don't know which is worse," my mom told my dad. "The boys were always so vocal about everything, but they were always obedient. Addie's quiet, but she does what she wants."

"She practices civil disobedience," my dad agreed.

"And I never know what's going on inside of her. The boys always let us know loud and clear if they were unhappy."

"They did." My dad laughed a little.

"The other kids weren't like this." My mom sounded sad and frustrated.

"The other kids weren't Addie," Dad answered. "She's her own person."

At least someone had that right.

CHAPTER 14

FEBRUARY

Sam Choi

In all the rush of getting ready for the wedding, I had somehow forgotten the fact that I wouldn't even be *at* the wedding. I mentioned that to Dad, and he grinned at me. "Don't worry, Sam. You'll be part of the luncheon and the reception and all the cleaning up afterward."

"Don't remind me."

So while (almost) everyone else was in the temple attending the one part of the day that actually mattered, Alex and I were sitting in the waiting room instead. We were hanging around the whole time just so we could be in a couple of pictures.

After all that work, we didn't even get to go inside.

Almost all of the Becketts were inside the temple. Ethan's older sister, Andrea, and her husband had flown in all the way from New York for the wedding. His other sister, Chloe, who was a few years younger than Alex, was sitting in the foyer with us. She kept twirling around in her red dress and telling anyone who would listen that she was a flower girl for the second time in a year.

"I think I'm dying," Alex told me. "Dying of boredom."

"Get used to it. The whole day is going to be like this."

As soon as I said that, Chloe let out a gasp. "There they are!"

Finally. Maybe the lack of sleep was getting to me, but it was cool to see my sister all dressed up and walking out with Ethan, who couldn't stop smiling and looking at her. I realized we were growing up. I felt—I don't know—sad and happy at the same time. Sad that she was leaving, happy that she had married someone who was a good guy.

Then Alex shoved me and said, "Hurry up, the sooner we get the group picture over with, the sooner we can eat," and I told him to quit shoving, that we were in the temple, and that ended the moment real fast.

• • •

In the reception line that night, Alex told everyone who would listen that he was starving. Mom finally told him to go get some food. When I moved to leave, too, she hissed at me, "*Not you!* Someone has to stay here!" Realizing how she sounded, she made a face. "Sorry. Can you wait a couple of minutes until Alex gets back?"

"All right." I knew I'd be stuck in line for awhile. Alex was going to take his sweet time now that he'd made his escape. I sighed and turned to talk to some cousin from Ethan's family. This reception was lasting forever, with no end in sight. My sister had committed to this guy for eternity, and right then it seemed like the rest of us had too.

Half an hour later, I was finally piling some food on a plate when someone came up next to me.

"Aren't you supposed to be standing in line?" It was Addie, all dressed up. It had been awhile since I'd seen her like that, since we're not in the same ward. She looked even better than usual. She never overdoes her makeup and hair like some other girls do. She doesn't have to because she's one of those girls who are good-looking to start with.

"Hey," I said. "They let me have a few minutes to eat. You wanna come sit by me?"

Addie nodded. I was relieved. Things were slowly getting back to normal after that night we went to the movies, and I'd made her mad. I told myself not to mention Rob.

"Did my brother Dave already come through the line?" she asked.

"Yeah, he was one of the first people here. It's been busy all night long. That must be what happens when both the bride and groom are from the same city."

"That's how it was at Dave and Avery's wedding reception too."

"How was Snoqualmie yesterday?" I hadn't been able to go because we'd had this fancy dinner the night before with Ethan's family.

"Not bad. Brook's getting better. Cody and I headed over to Blackhawk for most of the night. The snow was great."

"I can't believe this whole weekend is wasted," I complained. "Well, not wasted, but you know what I mean . . ."

"Mikey looks beautiful. Avery told me to notice everything, because Dave won't remember the details. The problem is that I don't know what I'm supposed to be noticing."

"You could make a list of all the refreshments." I pointed to her plate.

"I think she meant things like flowers and dresses. Do you know what kind of flowers these are?" She pointed to a bunch of red and white flowers standing in a short, square glass vase in the center of the table.

"Roses?"

Addie laughed. "Even *I* know those aren't roses."

"I know," I admitted. "My mom spent hours arranging them, and they'll probably get thrown away at the end of the night." I had an idea. "Hey, you should take some flowers for Avery. The reception is almost over, and I don't know what we're going to do with all this stuff anyway."

"Are you sure?"

"I'm positive. I'll help you take them to your car. Do you think she'd want some food too?"

"I don't want to steal from the reception," Addie protested.

"You'll be doing us a favor. The food tastes good now, but I don't want to be eating it all week."

I piled some of the refreshments on a plate. We waited for a moment until Mom's attention was diverted by the guests. I didn't think she would care about the food or the flowers, but I knew she wouldn't be too happy if she saw me leaving the building.

We snuck out to Addie's car. "Oh, no," she said, laughing. "You've got whipped cream on your tux."

"Shoot." She was right. I tried to wipe it off, but I could still see the smear. "My mom's going to kill me."

"Pin that flower you're wearing over the top of it," she suggested.

I tried, but I couldn't get the angle right. Finally, Addie pulled a roll of duct tape out of the car. "There's all kinds of random stuff in here from when my brothers drove this," she explained. She made a ball of tape and stuck it on my tux, then stuck the flower on top. It looked weird, but it stayed, barely, and hopefully no one would notice for the last few minutes of the reception.

"Thanks, Addie."

"Thanks for the food and everything. I bet Avery will like it." She climbed into her car and waved to me.

I waved back and returned to my place in the line. I felt much better. My stomach was full, and things were back to normal with Addie. Normal is such a good place to be.

• • •

"Is everyone ready?" Mikey called over her shoulder. She was standing on a chair and getting ready to throw her wedding bouquet. A bunch of girls crowded around her. Alex stood in the midst of them until Mom noticed and dragged him out, laughing.

"One, two, three . . ." The bouquet soared over Mikey's shoulder. My sister has a pretty good arm, especially considering she was throwing a bunch of flowers backwards without looking.

The bouquet flew right over all the girls, its long red ribbon streaming behind it. "Ohhhh," everyone said, and they turned to see who would catch the bouquet.

It sailed toward the refreshment table, toward the top tier of the wedding cake, which I guess the bride and groom had to save to eat on their first anniversary. (Yum. What says celebration like a frozen, one-year-old cake?) The bouquet started to fall, and I was sure it was going to knock over the cake. But someone standing near the table shot out an arm and grabbed the flowers just in time. She'd caught it with such force that a few of the petals rained down around the cake, but it was safe.

Mikey turned around to see who had caught the bouquet, and she started to smile. It was Ethan's mom, Sister Beckett.

• • •

Sister Beckett tried to give the bouquet back to Mikey, saying she hadn't meant to catch it, but Mikey told her to keep it. Ethan looked all kinds of uncomfortable about his mom catching the bouquet, and I didn't blame him. His parents were divorced and it probably didn't help that Ethan's dad was there to see it all. But Mikey and Mom and Sister Beckett and her boyfriend, Paul, all couldn't stop smiling.

"All right," Sister Beckett said, finally giving in. "I don't want to cause more of a scene than I already have. It's a beautiful bouquet. I love the white calla lilies and the red asters." I made a mental note to remember the names of the flowers so I could tell Addie. Of course, I forgot the names two seconds later, but at least I had tried.

It was time for Mikey and Ethan to leave. The two of them— Mr. and Mrs. Beckett—went around hugging everyone. When Mikey got to me, I felt kind of sad.

"You're Michaela Beckett now," I said to her. The name sounded like it belonged to someone I didn't even know.

"Everyone keeps telling me that."

"How does it feel to be Michaela Beckett, then?"

"Wonderful." She smiled at me. "But I'm still Michaela Choi, too."

"That's right," I told her. "Don't you forget it."

"She won't," Alex said, popping up next to us. "We won't let her." The two of us sandwiched her in a bone-crushing hug and she laughed and complained that we were ruining her hair. The wedding photographer snapped a picture, and then we finally let her go.

· · ·

Once Mikey and Ethan had driven off, the party died quickly. Mom sat down for the first time all night. She wasn't bawling, but both she and Dad had gotten emotional when Mikey and Ethan waved good-bye. Dad came and sat by Mom and put his arm around her. He whispered in her ear, and she started to laugh.

It took awhile to clean everything up. I wondered if Mikey and Ethan had any idea of all the work we were doing. I didn't think so. They'd been staring at each other all night long and hadn't noticed anyone else.

Finally, we were done. Our family and the Becketts said good-bye to the last few people who had stayed behind to help clean up. Then we walked out to the car. It felt different, not being a family of five anymore. We hadn't been for awhile, ever since Mikey went to college, but it still seemed strange. It seemed more permanent this time.

Mom hugged me before we got into the car. "Thank you so much, honey." My duct-taped flower fell off, but I caught it in one hand and she didn't notice. "You've been so much help with all of this. We could never have done it without you. What on earth are we going to do when you leave this fall?"

She looked like she might get emotional again, and I thought about telling her she might not have to worry about that after all. But of course I didn't. I didn't think it would make her feel much better.

MARCH

Caterina Giovanni

The night of the intervention, in between movies, we'd spent time in my room investigating. Our goal had been to find out more about Jenna without invading her privacy too much.

"I feel like a detective," Liz said, picking up a picture frame from the desk Jenna and I shared.

"Or a spy." Noelle was lying on my bed, looking up at the ceiling.

"I need to get out of here and play some volleyball," I said irritably, rummaging through my closet and looking for my favorite hoodie.

Noelle kept staring up at the glow-in-the-dark star stickers on the ceiling. They were Jenna's only other contribution to the room (other than her clothes, if you counted them). Jenna had spent an entire weekend arranging the stickers when she first moved in.

"So what have you detected?" Noelle asked Liz.

"Not much. She's by herself in both of the pictures. What do you think that means?"

"It could mean she's a loner," I suggested.

"We already knew that."

"What do you think the state of this closet might mean?" I shoved some more hangers to the side. "It's a mess. She has more clothes than anyone I've ever known."

"If she got mail, we'd know more, just from picking it up and bringing it back inside." Liz put down the picture frame. "But no one gets regular mail anymore. Unless it's their birthday and people send cards or packages. Wait—does anyone know when Jenna's birthday is?"

"I think she said it was in the summer." I'd found my green hoodie. It had been smashed so tightly in the crowded closet that it was wrinkled.

"So, we don't know much more about her except that she's been to the beach and to Washington, D.C., apparently by herself." Liz gestured to the pictures.

"Well, *someone* went with her. She didn't take the pictures," I pointed out.

"She could have asked a stranger."

"Wait," said Noelle, suddenly. She got up and went to lie down on Jenna's bed. "Turn out the lights," she commanded me.

"Um, Noelle, I don't think channeling her spirit is going to help."

"No, I'm serious. I think I might have detectified something interesting."

I turned out the lights. It took a second for our eyes to adjust, but in the winter darkness of 6:00 PM it was easy to see the stars above. There were so many of them.

Liz and I leaned back to look up. The stars looked cool, but I didn't think Noelle had "detectified" anything special. "It's pretty, but it doesn't tell us much. There aren't any words spelled out up there."

"She's mapped out the constellations," Noelle informed us. Noelle wanted to be a high school science teacher and a state champion volleyball coach someday. That's what she told everyone.

Anyway, she takes a lot of science classes, and she knows all about astronomy.

"Oh," Liz and I said at the same time. The three of us stared up at the fake night sky.

"That's cool," I admitted. "I hadn't noticed there was a pattern before."

"How could you miss that?" Noelle asked. "Look, it's arranged so that the Big Dipper is right over your head."

"You know I'm asleep before my head hits the pillow."

Noelle pointed out a few other constellations. "It's not to scale because she doesn't have enough space, but it's basically accurate."

"So she's interested in the stars, and she's smart," Liz deduced. "Is that really all we know about her?"

I sighed, depressed to think that Liz might be right.

• • •

Later that night we had our talk with Jenna. We told her that we'd give her a couple of days to talk to someone, like her parents, before we would do anything about the situation. I had to give a lot of credit to Noelle for how well it all went. It wasn't awesome, but it wasn't nearly as big a disaster as it could have been.

Jenna was defensive at first, but then toward the end, she cried a little and said she was sorry. She told us she had changed apartments in the middle of the year because she knew she had problems, and her old roommates had threatened to report her to the Honor Code office. But they never had. Instead, they avoided her altogether and made it clear she should try to find someplace else to live. She told us the group she drank with was a bunch of people she'd met "through a friend." From some other things she said that night, I assumed it was the same "friend" who had been in our room with her that night in January. She said she didn't blame us if we hated her.

"We don't hate you," Noelle told her sincerely, and Liz and I agreed.

"You probably don't want me to live with you next year, right?"

I was honest. "We want to have you live with us, as long as you don't break the rules, and as long as you talk to someone. We like you, Jenna. We want to get to know you better. Maybe that can happen if we get all this other stuff out of the way."

"Okay," she said. "I'll talk to someone before next week. I promise."

She looked like she was about to cry, and she turned toward our room, but that's when Noelle saved the day. "Come have some of these," she said, nudging the pan of treats closer to Jenna. "And hey, have you been holding out on me? Are you a physical science major too? I saw the stars in your room when I was talking to Cate tonight."

Jenna paused. "Yeah, I am."

"Why haven't we been studying together? What classes are you taking this semester?"

After that night, Jenna started hanging out with us more. Not a ton, but more than she had been. We tried to include her. We were gone a lot for our intramural team, but she started coming to our games and sitting in the stands with anyone from our ward who happened to show up. It turned out she and Noelle were taking the same class from the same professor but at different times, so they started working on their assignments together. Jenna wanted to be a high school teacher, too, so she and Noelle would be going through the whole earth science secondary education program together and everything.

She also kept her promise about talking to someone. We assumed she would call her parents, but she ended up talking to the bishop on Sunday. He called us later that night and asked if we could all come to meet with him in his office on Thursday at 5:00 PM.

We all had classes that day, so we converged at his office from our separate parts of campus. I got there last, or almost last. Noelle and Liz were already waiting in the hall, but Jenna was nowhere in sight.

"Where's Jenna?" I asked them.

"No idea," Liz answered.

"Hello, ladies," the bishop said, opening the door. "It looks like you're all here. Come on in."

"We're missing someone," I said, pointing out the obvious. "Jenna's not here."

"She called a minute ago to say she was stuck on campus, studying, and couldn't make it," Bishop Corwin told us.

"Oh." So it was just the three of us and the bishop. We exchanged looks as we went into his office and sat down.

"Jenna feels uncomfortable and embarrassed," the bishop said, after he'd shaken our hands and offered us chairs. "I'm not surprised she found a reason to be absent tonight. But I'm glad the three of you are here. You've handled this very well so far, but I wondered if you might want to talk about it too. It would be better if Jenna were here, of course, but if there are things we can discuss without her, we should take this opportunity."

We asked the bishop a few questions about what we should do. Bishop Corwin asked us to tell him about our concerns regarding Jenna, so we did. He said we were handling things well by treating her like we would a sister or a friend. He also said we were right to tell her she had to take care of her problems, and added that she was a good person going through a hard time. Without revealing anything, he also said that she had had some struggles in her life and that we should try to be compassionate, but firm.

It was nice to know we weren't the only ones looking out for Jenna.

"What about her parents?" I asked Bishop Corwin. "Do they know?"

"Yes, they know. But that's all I can tell you without betraying a confidence."

"Oh, okay," I said. I had other questions about that—*What are they going to do about it? Aren't they even going to come visit her or check on her?*—but at least now I knew they had some clue about what was going on with their daughter.

"I'm glad Jenna ended up in your apartment," Bishop Corwin said at the end of the interview.

"So am I," I said automatically since he was looking right at me. We took our turns shaking his hand again and left. It had been a short conversation, and I didn't know exactly what it had accomplished, but at least it seemed like a small step in the right direction.

"Did you mean that?" Liz asked me as we walked home. "Are you really glad Jenna ended up in our apartment?"

"I don't know," I admitted. "Ask me later when the semester is over and we've figured everything out. What about you?"

"I feel the same way you do."

"Me too," agreed Noelle.

It was already dark, and we walked down the white band of sidewalk in silence for a few seconds. A guy came toward us, and the three of us split to let him pass. Then we moved back together again.

"What do you think the struggles are that Bishop Corwin mentioned?" I asked. "The ones we already know about, or different ones?"

"I wonder what's going on with her family," Liz said. "Why else would she talk to the bishop first and not her parents?"

"I think you're right," Noelle agreed. "Have you noticed she hardly ever mentions her family? I know she has parents and a sister, but that's it. I don't even know their names."

We were coming up behind another figure. This time, the person was walking slowly in the same direction we were. I gestured to Noelle to be quiet. Even though the person was far away, somehow I could tell it was Jenna. She was walking home from campus alone in the dark. Not the smartest thing to do, even at BYU–Idaho.

"Jenna!" I called out. The figure startled, stopped, and turned around. "It's us! Wait up!"

We hurried to catch up with her. She looked embarrassed but also determined to avoid blame. "Oh, hi, you guys. Sorry I missed the meeting. This study group came up that I couldn't miss."

Liz was quick to let her off the hook. "Bishop Corwin told us. Did you get a lot done?"

"Yeah. There's a test tomorrow in my math class, and I think I'm better prepared now." We walked a few more steps in an awkward silence. She had to know that we'd been talking about her, but it didn't seem like any of us wanted to go there.

"So, what's going on this weekend?" Jenna asked us.

It was a perfect change of subject. "Oh, yeah, I've been meaning to ask you," I said. "Noelle and I are thinking we might go to that sleigh ride and dinner activity." Noelle was involved with the Outdoor Activities group, and they were always planning fun events.

"We're going to take dates," Noelle added.

"Do you want to go with us? I'm thinking about asking Chase, and Noelle's taking Biology Class Boy"—Noelle made a face at me— "I mean Noah."

"What about you? Are you going?" Jenna asked Liz.

"I'm driving home Friday afternoon. My nephew is being blessed this weekend."

"The activity is going to be a lot of fun," Noelle said. "Trust me. And it doesn't cost too much either. You should come. You could bring that guy you went on the date with last weekend."

"Okay. It does sound fun." Jenna's voice sounded fake-happy, like she was trying the tone on for size. I didn't want to tell her that it didn't fit. At least she was making an effort.

"Great."

"I think I'll bring someone else," Jenna said. "There's this guy in my math class—he was the one who wanted to study this afternoon. I don't want to go out with the same guy too many times."

"Really?" I asked. That was news to me, especially after the late-night, boy-in-our-room incident. I still couldn't figure out what was going on between the two of them. Although, when I thought about it, she *did* go out with other people and not just him.

"You know that I'm writing to a missionary, right?"

I could tell Noelle and Liz were surprised, too, but we all tried to play it cool.

"No, I didn't, actually," Liz said. "Is he from home?"

"He is. We went to high school together. We were best friends until our senior year, and then we started dating. He left in the fall."

"Where's he serving?"

"In France."

"Oh, which mission?"

"Um, Paris?"

"My older brother is in the Bordeaux France Mission," Liz explained. "That's why I was wondering. They wouldn't run into each other, then, if your boyfriend is in Paris."

"Probably not," Jenna said. "His name's Mark. Mark Lowry."

"So . . . what's he like?"

"How come you don't have any pictures of him up in our room?" I asked her curiously. It seemed like most girls I knew who were writing seriously to guys on missions liked to make the fact known.

Jenna looked surprised. "Well, it's too hard to look at them all the time. I don't know if that makes sense, but that's how I feel."

"I can see that," I said. I guess I could. I wouldn't know. I'm not the type of girl to be all hung up on a missionary. I didn't say that, though, because then Noelle and Liz would tease me about Steve and say that I would miss him like crazy.

"But you have a picture of him somewhere, right? We want to see what he looks like," Noelle said mischievously.

"I'll show you sometime." Jenna smiled. "He's cute, and he's so sweet. I bet you would all like him. He played basketball for our high school, and he's totally hilarious." She sighed. "I miss him a *lot*."

We all agreed he sounded great.

Most girls who tell you they "have a missionary" have pictures of him everywhere. I even went to one apartment in our ward where the girl had a picture of the guy in every room—on the fridge in the kitchen, on top of the television in the living room, everywhere.

I knew another girl who had a picture of her missionary on her cell phone display, and every time the phone rang, it played their song, which was "God Be with You Till We Meet Again." Seriously.

That kind of thing is too cheesy for me. I was glad Jenna wasn't like that about Mark.

We continued on our way home together, talking more about Mark and Biology Class Boy, and then Steve picked that exact moment to text me a message on my cell phone, so of course we had to talk about him too.

We were just four college roommates walking home and talking about guys. It was nice. As we crossed the parking lot and walked toward our apartment, I noticed that a few real stars were becoming visible in the night sky. It made me sad to think of Jenna lying in bed at night, looking up at the fake stars when the real ones were right outside.

CHAPTER 16

MARCH

Addie Sherman

I'm the only teenager in America without a cell phone. Not having one drives me crazy all the time, but the day I got a message from the office during chemistry was the worst. I'd been distracting myself with thoughts of snowboarding when an office aide came into the room with a message for a student. I knew it had to be for me, even before Mr. Hughes beckoned me to the front of the room and gave me the square piece of fluorescent green paper. The office staff always uses that paper for messages. They must want to get our attention—or damage our eyesight.

I squinted at the note. "Please call your mother after class. You may use the school phone." My heart jumped into my throat. This had to be about Avery. Had something bad happened?

When the bell finally rang, I raced down the hall to the office with my note. The secretary slid the phone toward me, and I dialed my mom's work number as fast as I could.

My mom answered. "Is everything okay with Avery?" I asked, before she'd had a chance to say more than "hello."

"I should have realized you'd be worried about that." My mom sounded repentant. "Avery's fine. I'm sorry that I scared you."

"Then why did you have me come to the office to call you?" Annoyance quickly replaced relief. Couldn't this, whatever it was, have waited until I got home from snowboarding?

"I wanted to catch you before you left with Sam and Rob and Cody, because I don't think you're going snowboarding today. Mrs. Bryant gave me a call earlier this afternoon, Addie."

This was not a conversation I wanted to have standing in the school office. I wasn't going to say, "Oh, so you know I'm failing?" in front of all the other students, or even, "Mrs. Bryant is an evil, evil person."

My mom didn't notice my silence, or didn't care.

"Addie, she's worried. She's going on her maternity leave soon, and she wanted to talk to me before she did because she's concerned you could fail her class. She said you failed the last assignment and don't seem to be caring very much anymore. She also told me you're way below a B."

I stayed silent.

My mom sighed. "We have to talk about this later tonight. And you know you can't go snowboarding anymore. You didn't hold up your end of the bargain."

I felt something crumple inside of me, and I just wanted to get out of the office before the outside matched up. "I'll be right home."

"Actually, Dave called. He was wondering if one of us could come over to stay with Avery this afternoon, since her mom can't make it," Mom said to me. "I can't get away from work for an hour or two, so we need you to go there right now. But this will be the last time we have you go over there for awhile. Passing your classes is important."

"It's about time I didn't have to babysit her anymore."

"Addie—" Mom warned.

I wasn't in the mood for whatever else she was going to say.

So for the first time in my life, I hung up on my mom. It felt really, really good for about five seconds, about as long as it took me to walk out of the office, and then I felt even worse. I headed out to the parking lot to find the guys and give them the bad news. They were probably already loaded up in Rob's car, ready to go.

Sure enough, I didn't even make it halfway to my car before they pulled up next to me.

"Addie, where have you been? We're going to be late!" Rob rolled down the window. "Get in the car, and we'll drive you over to get your stuff!"

Cody was grinning from the front seat, and Sam reached across the back to open the door for me.

It was too much. "I can't go with you guys." To my embarrassment, I started crying.

"What happened?" Sam asked, staring at me. "Are you okay?"

"I'm fine. My mom found out about my grades, that's all." I tried to smile and shrug. "I should have known it would happen eventually. I'll see you guys later."

"Addie—" I heard Rob call, but I waved again and kept walking. They didn't follow me. The thing about guys is that they will usually leave you alone when you act like that's what you want. And they don't make you talk through everything. I did not want to talk through anything, ever. Especially not this.

I started my car and pulled out through the open parking slot in front of me, not looking back once to see what Rob, Sam, and Cody were doing. I wasn't crying anymore, and that felt worse. I almost wanted the tears to start again.

•   •   •

Although I was tempted to get on Interstate 405 and drive straight out of town, I resisted the urge and drove over to Avery and Dave's house instead. At least I could postpone confronting my mom for a couple of hours. Hopefully, Avery would be busy today with a big assignment to work on for one of her classes. I needed there to be no drama. No stupid invitations to make. No unexplained almost-tears. No bossing me around with errands for the reunion.

No such luck. I had barely walked through the door when I heard Avery call, "Addie, is that you?"

"Yup." I walked into the family room. Avery was sitting on the couch, as always, and she held out a piece of paper to me. I took it from her and looked at it. Great. It was one of the invitations we'd sent out to the reunion for her friends.

"Look!" Avery said, close to tears. "I just realized the invitations say, *reonion!* Not *reunion!* And they've already been sent out to every-one!"

I don't know what happened to me. I'm not a mean person. But I honestly couldn't care about the misspelled invitations. After all the stress of the day, the fact that they said "reonion" didn't seem tragic. It *did* seem ironic that she'd spent all that time worrying about how they looked and hadn't noticed the spelling was wrong. I started laughing.

"It's not funny!" Avery told me.

"Yes, it is."

"I'm an English major! This is humiliating." She sounded angry now instead of sad.

"No one will even care. They'll still come and have fun, Avery. The invitations don't matter that much."

"How can you say that? After all the work we put into them?" She paused. "We'll have to redo them."

No way. "You have to be kidding me. There's no way I'm helping with that."

"But I was sure you would! I was all excited when Dave said you were coming today because you're the one who knows how to do this!"

"You were excited I was coming today," I repeated.

"Yes!"

And then I let loose. "Avery, do you even know *anything* about my life? Fridays I go snowboarding. *Every* Friday. It's my favorite thing in the world. And you know about the deal with my parents and my grades and snowboarding. If I'm here on a Friday, it means something is wrong, but you don't even care about that, you didn't even ask what had happened." Avery was getting that look on her face, the sad one that makes me worried, and I started to feel bad. I tried to calm down. I handed her back the invitation she'd given me. "Anyway, I'm not going to redo them, and I'm not coming back after today. I'm failing English. My parents aren't letting me go up to Snoqualmie anymore, and they're going to try to work things out so I don't have to come here either."

"But I thought you were keeping your grades up," Avery said softly. "You told everyone you were doing fine."

"Well, I wasn't, and now everyone knows the truth. I'm sorry. I hope that doesn't mess things up for you and Dave too much."

"It doesn't matter. The doctor actually took me off bed rest a couple of days ago." She didn't look at me when she said it.

I was shocked. "Why didn't you tell me? Did you tell my mom?"

"No. I didn't tell anyone but Dave."

"Then why are we all still bending over backwards for you?" I felt angry and betrayed all over again. "Why would the two of you lie to us?"

"Why would you lie to your mom about your grades?" she shot back, sounding more like the old Avery. Then she said softly, "Dave and I didn't lie to you. No one asked, and I wanted people to keep coming over. I'm still nervous about being alone."

We looked at each other for a few seconds, but I couldn't take it. I don't like confrontation. "I think I'd better go home," I muttered, picking up my bag. Avery was still quiet. "Tell Dave I can't believe that he—never mind."

What a couple of liars Avery and I were.

I drove around for an hour before I went home. I thought about telling my parents what had happened and the truth about Dave and Avery but decided, as usual, to keep my mouth shut. I listened to what my parents had to say about my English grade, agreed that they were right and the punishment was fair, and nodded my head at all the right times. Then I went upstairs to my room and left them to talk about me again. But I didn't even try to listen this time. What could they say that I hadn't already heard?

· · ·

The next morning, the doorbell rang. "Addie, can you get that?" my mom called from her room. "I'm talking to Dave on the phone."

Oh, boy. I didn't want to know the details of *that* conversation. I went to the front door, expecting to find a ward member or neighbor. Cody stood there instead.

"Who is it?" my mom called.

"It's for me," I called back. I didn't invite Cody in, but stepped outside and closed the door behind me. "Hey," I said, gesturing for him to sit on the porch bench. I sat down next to him.

"What's up?" Cody asked.

"Nothing."

"So are you okay or what?"

"I'm fine. I mean, I'm not fine about the snowboarding, but there's nothing I can do about it. I've been trying to pass my classes, and I'm just too stupid."

My mom opened the door. "Hi, Cody."

"Hey, Mrs. Sherman."

"Addie, you can have five minutes, all right?"

"Okay." I was surprised she'd given me that long. I was willing to bet it was because no one could resist the puppy-dog look Cody had perfected and was currently using on her.

But the look didn't go away when she shut the door. That was weird. Was Cody actually sad? I hadn't seen that before. "Cody, is everything all right?" I braced myself, certain he would slug me for even asking such a thing. But he didn't.

"You know that girl? The one who asked me out last Saturday?"

"Of course. Megan. You guys had fun, right?"

"No." Cody stopped. I waited for him to say more. "Turns out she actually likes Sam instead of me. The whole time we were on the date, she was asking me about Sam."

"I'm sorry, Cody." I was. I knew how *that* felt.

"You know what else? Sam doesn't even like her. He likes you."

"What?" I asked. "Cody, you're making that up." My heart was pounding.

"Well, I don't know if it's true anymore, but I bet he still does. He wanted to take you to the Valentine's dance, but he figured out that you liked someone else." Cody paused. "Don't tell him I told you that or he'll kill me."

"Okay," I agreed. We sat in silence for a few seconds. "We both had horrible weeks, huh?"

"I think I win."

"I think *I* win. I can't go snowboarding for the rest of the season, remember?"

"All right," Cody said. "You do win."

There wasn't much to say after that, but it was nice not to be alone and feeling depressed. We sat there together for a minute before Cody told me he'd see me later and left. I went inside and back up to my room and flopped down on my bed. In spite of the fact that it had been the worst couple of days ever, I was smiling to myself. Cody thought Sam liked me.

A spark of happiness flared up inside of me.

Then the spark died again, as I realized that Sam liked the Addie who was good, not the Addie who lied to her parents and was mean to Avery. Not the one who seemed to be showing up more and more lately.

CHAPTER 17

MARCH

Sam Choi

It was weird going snowboarding without Addie on Friday night. All of us missed her—me, Rob, Brook, and Cody. I think we all wished we hadn't left her behind the way we did, but we didn't know what else to do.

Without Addie, it felt like one of the most important parts of snowboarding was missing. It was like going camping and realizing you'd forgotten your flashlight. You could work around it, but things would be a lot better with it.

I called her the next morning to see how things were going. Her parents were still ticked about the whole homework thing, and she wasn't doing much besides studying. She said she wouldn't even be going over to her brother's house to help out anymore, although I felt like there was more to that story than she was telling me. We talked for a few minutes and then hung up. I thought about going over to visit her, but I didn't know if she would want me to do that.

When Monday came around and Addie wasn't in school, I decided to pick up her English homework and use it as an excuse to go to her house and see her. Even though Addie was a junior and I was a senior, we both had Mrs. Bryant for English. I had her for AP, and Addie had her for junior English. I figured it wouldn't be too hard to get her assignment. Then her parents couldn't get mad if I came over to visit.

After school, I went into Mrs. Bryant's room, but she wasn't there. Instead, there was an older man sitting at her desk, going through some of Mrs. Bryant's stuff. That was weird. Do teachers spy on each other and steal each other's lesson plans?

"Hello," he said. "Can I help you?"

"Uh, no. That's okay. I was looking for Mrs. Bryant."

"That's me." He smiled at my confusion. "I'm Mr. Thomas. I'm taking over for her during her maternity leave, starting tomorrow. She's actually at the hospital right now, having her baby. She left at lunchtime."

"Oh," I said. "She told us we'd be getting a sub pretty soon. You used to teach here, right?"

"Yes, I did."

"I think you taught my sister. Her name's Michaela Choi."

He smiled. "I did. She was an excellent student and very likable."

"That's her." I get that a lot when I ask if people know my sister. It wasn't like Mikey was a superstar valedictorian prom queen, but everyone liked her, especially teachers.

"I went to her wedding reception just last month," Mr. Thomas said, surprising me. "She and Ethan Beckett were both students of mine. I thought you looked familiar—I must have seen you there."

I felt bad, but I didn't remember him. There had been a lot of people going through the line that night. "Oh, right," I said. I cleared my throat awkwardly. "So, I was wondering. Do you happen to know what the homework was for junior English tonight? I have a friend who is sick, and I wanted to take it over to her."

"I can try to find out. Mrs. Bryant left some notes for me." He rummaged through them for a few minutes, then pulled a piece of paper from a stack at the corner of the desk. "Here it is. It looks like it's a prompt for a short essay she wants them to write. It says here that the assignment is due tomorrow."

An essay. Addie would love that. Maybe I shouldn't take it over to her house after all.

Ever since I went on splits with the missionaries, I'd been riding my bike to school when the weather was decent. I went out to the bike rack, shoved the assignment into the pocket of my hoodie and rode to Addie's house. If her parents stuck to the no-snowboarding rule, maybe I could talk Addie into going bike riding with me sometime instead. I grinned to myself, picturing it. "Hey, you want to ride bikes?" We'd be like a couple of little neighborhood kids again.

• • •

Mrs. Sherman answered the door. I started talking right away in case she was going to say I couldn't come inside. "I brought Addie's English homework."

Mrs. Sherman smiled. "Come on in, Sam," she said. She called up the stairs for Addie and then started into the kitchen. Over her shoulder, she called back, "Addie has laryngitis, so she can't talk very well."

"Oh, okay."

"Hey, Sam," someone squeaked from the stairs. I turned around. Addie looked normal, but her voice sure wasn't. She sounded like a squeaky Muppet character who'd been sucking helium from a balloon. It was that high. I tried to fight away the smile that kept twisting the corners of my mouth.

"It sounds worse than it is," Addie told me. "I don't feel that bad."

I couldn't help it. I cracked up.

Addie looked annoyed. "What? There's nothing I can do about it."

Hearing her grumpy tone with her high squeaky voice was even funnier. Even she realized it and started to grin. "Oh, you're right. It *is* funny. What do you want, anyway?"

"I brought over your homework from English," I told her, pulling it out of my pocket. The paper was smashed, but I unfolded it and smoothed it out.

"My mom already called the school and went over to pick it up this morning." Addie sighed. "She's not taking any chances."

"Oh."

"But that was nice of you."

"No problem. Do you want me to bring your assignment tomorrow if you're not there?"

"That would be great. I definitely won't be going to school if I still sound like this. Can you imagine what Cody would say?"

I grinned. I could.

"So what's new at school?"

"Nothing. Well, Mrs. Bryant is gone. She's having her baby. I met the sub today when I picked up your assignment. He seemed cool. He used to teach there."

"I hope he's easier than Mrs. Bryant."

"Me, too."

We were both quiet for a minute. Talking about English was dangerously close to talking about snowboarding, and I knew that was not going to go well. I tried to think of a smooth way to change the subject, but all I came up with was, "I hope you feel better soon."

"Thanks. I'll see you tomorrow, right?"

"Yeah."

"I'd invite you to stay longer, but I don't want you to get sick too."

"I should go home and get started on my homework anyway. All the AP teachers are loading us up to get us ready for the tests in May."

"Good luck," Addie squeaked. I waved at her and went back

outside. I picked up my bike from where it was lying on the grass and started riding toward home.

Going up the hill toward my neighborhood, I saw the missionaries riding their bikes ahead of me. They weren't going very fast. Elder Smellder was probably slowing them down. I bet their scriptures weren't helping, either. Scriptures are heavy.

I passed them halfway up the hill and called out to them as I did. They both lifted a hand to wave at me and kept on going up the hill. I came to the top and coasted down the other side. I'd totally wasted them.

If I went on a mission, at least I'd have killer biking skills. That's important, right?

CHAPTER 18

MARCH

Caterina Giovanni

For awhile, it felt like we had weathered the storm and things were going to be fine. We hung out with Jenna a lot. She visited with the bishop often. I heard back from the research center in Seattle and had been hired as an assistant for the summer. Biology Class Boy and Noelle were officially dating. Steve was calling me more and more.

Then Noelle told us she wasn't sure things were going so well with Jenna after all. "I think she's been skipping classes. Whenever we do our homework together, she doesn't have a clue about what's going on. I know she hasn't been going to *that* class, at least."

"Then where is she going?" I asked. Jenna still got up early every morning and left the apartment before the rest of us did. We all assumed she'd been going to class.

"I have no idea."

"Do you think she's going to pass?"

"I don't know. I don't think so. That's one class you can't miss if you want to know what's going on."

Once again, we were at a loss about what to do. Everyone except for me had a date that night, so I stayed home and finished a paper and felt sorry for myself until Chase called. He asked me if I wanted to come over to their apartment and hang out for awhile. They were having a bunch of people over to watch some of the NCAA basketball games. I told him I'd be right there.

I was about to leave when my cell phone rang. It was Jenna, sounding like she was about to cry. "Can you come get me, Cate?"

"Where are you? Aren't you on a date?"

"I was, but I think I'm ready to come home now."

"I'll come get you. Oh, wait. I don't have a car." Somehow we had both forgotten that minor detail. "Just a second. Let me see if Liz or Noelle left their keys."

"Okay."

I was in luck. Noelle had left her keys right on the kitchen table. She and Liz had both told me that if I needed to, I could borrow their cars in an emergency. I'd never taken either of them up on the offer before. I didn't know if this qualified as an emergency, but it seemed to have definite emergency potential.

"I found Noelle's keys." I could hear Jenna's sigh of relief. "Where are you?"

She gave me the address of an apartment complex, and I was off to the rescue. I didn't even think to call Chase to tell him that I wasn't going to be able to come over.

• • •

It wasn't hard to find Jenna. She was standing under a streetlamp right inside the parking lot. A guy was with her. I recognized him as I pulled up next to the curb. He was the one who had been in our room that night when I'd come home late. He was arguing with Jenna, standing close to her, but not touching her. She was arguing back. He shrugged and turned away as I opened the door and started to get out.

Before I could, Jenna ran over to the passenger side and climbed in. She looked shaky.

"Are you okay?" I asked her. I pulled away from the curb and didn't look back. I wanted to get her out of there and away from him, whoever he was.

"Yes."

It was obvious she was trying not to cry. I drove for a few seconds without speaking, but crazy thoughts ran through my head about date rape or something awful. I had to know the truth. "Jenna, what happened? That guy—the one you were arguing with—did he—"

She cut me off. "No." Now she was flat-out bawling. "I need to go home."

"I'll get us there as fast as I can."

"No, I mean, I need to go *home*. Back to Utah."

"Oh."

I couldn't get anything more out of her until we got back to the apartment. Liz and Noelle were back by then. As Jenna went crying past them, they gave me a what-on-earth-is-going-on look, and I answered with an I-have-no-clue look. I followed Jenna into our room and closed the door.

"Jenna, I'm worried about you."

"I need to go home," she said again.

"What's happened?"

"I'm not strong enough to do this on my own. I need to go home."

Gradually, the whole story came out. She'd run into this guy, Sean, the day before, and he'd wanted her to hang out with him again. She knew she shouldn't, because he was one of the ones in the group of friends who got into trouble, but she decided to go anyway. Once she was there, she'd made some mistakes, and she knew she had to leave. That made Sean mad, which was why they'd been arguing when I pulled up in Noelle's car.

Jenna didn't smell like she'd been drinking, but she'd been gone long enough to get into a few different kinds of trouble.

"I'm so stupid. I always go with the guys who make me feel horrible about myself and who treat me bad. That's the only kind of guy who likes me, anyway."

"That's not true. Remember that guy from your math class you took on the sleigh ride? And I think Brett liked you, too. So there's two nice guys who were interested in you."

"That's the problem. When I meet someone cool, I get scared that I'm going to mess it up, so I don't dare go out with them more than once or twice. I know they'd never like me if they really knew me."

"Mark cares about you, and he's a great guy."

That made her cry harder. She said something I couldn't understand. "What?" I asked.

She said it again. "He's not even real."

"What do you mean?"

"Mark. He's not even real. I made him up."

"You made him up? But what about the picture you showed us?" She had shown us a picture of her with a cute guy at a football game. She was leaning close to him and smiling and he had his arm around her. It had looked real to me.

"That's a friend from high school. And he is named Mark. But he goes to school at BYU. He's not on a mission, and we've never dated. I invented all of that."

"Why?" I didn't understand. "It's not like any of us have boyfriends, except Noelle."

"I don't know. I guess I wanted to feel like someone like that would want to be with me."

"Oh, Jenna." I didn't know what to say. Finally I told her, "You need to give yourself a break."

"No." She wasn't crying anymore. "I've given myself too many breaks. I need to get tougher. I need to sort this all out before things get worse. But I don't think I can do it here. I know I can't do it on my own."

That hurt my feelings a little, even though I knew this wasn't about me. Couldn't she tell we'd been trying? "Jenna, you don't have to do it on your own. We're all here for you. The bishop is worried about you too."

"I know. But it's not enough right now."

I could understand that. "Okay. Are you going to call your parents?"

She nodded, picking up her cell phone.

"I'll give you some privacy, then."

I could hear Jenna say "Mom?" as I closed the door behind me. I went to tell Noelle and Liz that we were about to lose a roommate.

I wondered if they would feel like failures. I did.

• • •

Jenna's parents arrived the very next morning. After I'd spent the past couple of months thinking there must be something wrong with them, their normalness was both surprising and comforting to me. They looked like anyone else's mom and dad who were worn out from driving all night to help their daughter. And they were both there. That meant that they cared, didn't it? We'd been wrong about her family all along.

I was the only one awake when they arrived. In fact, I'd never gone to sleep. Jenna had fallen asleep after talking to her parents on the phone, but then she'd woken up at 4:00 AM to start packing. She apologized for getting up so early, but I didn't mind since I'd been tossing and turning anyway. I got up and offered to help her. She'd saved some of her boxes from moving in. They were folded up at the back of our closet, so we pulled them out and taped them back together.

I hadn't kept any boxes, and I didn't think Noelle or Liz had either. Had Jenna always known she would be leaving soon?

Neither of us said much as we filled the boxes with her clothes.

I'd been complaining for a long time about all the clothes she had, but it didn't seem to take that long to pack them all up.

· · ·

Noelle, Liz, and I felt awkward being around Jenna and her parents, but we hung around the apartment that morning anyway. We didn't want Jenna to leave without any of us there to see her off.

It was weird saying good-bye to Jenna. We all helped carry her boxes to the car, and then we stood there not knowing what to do. She didn't make a move to hug us, so we didn't either. She waved to us, said, "See you guys later," and climbed quickly into the backseat of the car. Her parents said good-bye. And then they were gone.

It was freezing outside, but we all stood there until the car was out of sight. The parking lot was deserted, and none of the apartments showed any signs of life. It was only nine o'clock on a Saturday morning and it didn't look like anyone else in our complex was even awake.

"I wonder what Mark will think when he hears about all this," Liz said. "Do you think he knows about everything that's been going on with her?"

I looked up in surprise. Somehow I had forgotten to tell them about Mark when I was explaining what had happened and why Jenna was leaving.

"He's not real," I told Liz and Noelle.

Their faces looked the way mine had a few hours before.

"What?" Noelle asked.

"Last night, when we were talking, Jenna admitted she'd made him up. There *is* a Mark from high school, but he's not on a mission in France. He goes to BYU, and they're not dating. They're just friends."

"Why would she do that?" Liz asked.

"I don't know. I think she wanted to feel like someone loved her and cared about her."

"That's sad," Noelle said.

The three of us turned and walked back into the apartment. It already seemed emptier. Noelle went over and opened up the cupboard Jenna had used. There was a little more shelf space, but not much. She hadn't had too many dishes.

I opened the fridge. There were a few items marked "J"—milk, peanut butter (which for some reason Jenna liked kept cold), eggs. There was a box of her favorite chocolate cereal in the cupboard.

"This is weird," Liz said as the three of us started getting out bowls and cereal for breakfast. None of us reached for Jenna's cereal. I wondered if it would sit there all year, like a monument or a marker. *Jenna was here.* It didn't seem like much.

"It's like Jenna never happened," Noelle said.

"Do you think she'll be back next year?" I asked.

"Or will she be put on academic probation for not finishing the semester?" Liz wondered.

None of us had any answers. It seemed like we never had, for Jenna. "This is depressing," I said, and they both agreed. We finished our cereal in silence. I remembered the time Jenna had gone grocery shopping with us, and we'd all picked out our cereal. That had only been about a month ago. It seemed longer.

Once we finished eating, Noelle suggested we play volleyball, but I was too tired from the night before. "I think I'm going back to bed. I didn't sleep much last night." They left, and I headed to the room that I now had all to myself.

The sight of Jenna's bare mattress and empty half of the closet was disheartening. I guess she hadn't taken up too much space after all.

I didn't go to sleep right away. First, I put one of my extra blankets on Jenna's bed. Then I dusted off the desk and rearranged the closet so that my things were more spread out, and it looked less empty.

I left the stars up.

CHAPTER 19

END OF MARCH

Addie Sherman

Every Friday of that long month of March, I tormented myself by listening to the snow reports from Snoqualmie Pass. I knew from the reports that the last weekend of March was the last weekend they planned to stay open. It had been an unusually warm winter, and it didn't sound like it would be a very great closing weekend. Because there wasn't much snowpack, the snow would be bad, and the weather was supposed to be warm, which would make it even more slushy.

I still wanted to go so bad it almost made me cry.

I was on my way out the door for school when my mom stopped me. She was carrying my snowboard. Before I could say anything, she held it out to me. "I heard this is going to be the last weekend. I think you should go."

It had to be a trick. I'd turned in all my English assignments for the past month and was (barely) passing again, but I'd still broken the agreement.

My mom held out my snowboard again. "I'm serious, honey."

"What changed your mind?"

"Avery talked me into it," she said. "For someone so quiet, she can sometimes surprise me with how much she's willing to talk."

"She surprises me too."

"I think you should be able to go one last time." My mom held out my board again. This time I took it.

"Thanks, Mom," I said, and I started to grin.

I smiled all the way to school, where I ran down the hall to Sam's locker before stopping at my own.

He turned to see me, and his face lit up. "You're coming, aren't you?" he said before I could even tell him what had happened. I nodded. He hugged me right there in the middle of the hall, quickly, but not so quickly that Cody, who was coming our way, couldn't yell out, "Get a room, Sam and Addie!" We broke apart, laughing, and not quite meeting each other's eyes.

I couldn't wait, couldn't wait, *couldn't wait* for school to get out.

● ● ●

The snow was terrible. It was really slushy, and I could see patches of earth on parts of the run. But I didn't care. I leaned back on the lift and tipped my head to the last of the afternoon sun.

"Watch out," Sam warned me. "You're going to fall asleep and then ride right back down the lift, and you'll never even snowboard at all. You'll nap your way through the whole night."

"It feels so good to be back up here again. I can't believe it's only been a month. It feels like forever."

"It does," Sam said quietly. We rode for a few seconds in silence. Then he turned to me and said, "You owe me an apology."

"For what?"

"For the past month. I had to ride with Cody every single time on the lifts while you were gone."

"I owe you an apology for something else too," I told him. "I'm sorry for being so hard to talk to lately. It just hurt a lot that I couldn't come with you guys. I'm sorry about all of that."

"It's okay. I'm glad you're back." He smiled at me in a completely friendly way.

I had realized something the night Cody told me that Sam liked me: I didn't care about Rob and Brook anymore. I cared about Sam and me. It had been happening gradually over the past few months, or maybe since we'd met in elementary school. Who knew? All I knew was that things had changed, especially lately, but I hadn't wanted to acknowledge it. I didn't want to be hurt again so soon after realizing that Rob didn't feel the same way I did. I knew deep down being rejected by Sam would cut much deeper and hurt a lot worse.

I looked over at Sam. I'd sat next to him hundreds of times, but lately, every time I was near him, I felt this strange feeling of wanting more, of having to physically restrain myself from reaching out for his hand, or moving closer. Today was no different.

Sam noticed me watching him. "What's up?" he asked me.

Cody must have been wrong. It didn't seem like Sam liked me as more than a friend anymore. It had taken me too long to recognize how I felt about Sam, and I'd missed my chance.

I owed Sam another apology, for not realizing that I liked him in time. Now it was too late. Maybe I owed myself the apology, instead.

But I was grateful to have the chance to go snowboarding once more. It was more than I thought I would get. I owed Avery big time. I wondered what she had said to my mom to get her to change her mind. I was also glad Sam was still my friend. At least I hadn't lost that.

Sam was still waiting for me to answer him. I pulled off my hat and held it out. "Looks like this is it," I told Sam. The hat was the hideous star-spangled beanie I'd worn back in January, the day Brook had come snowboarding with us for the first time, the hat Dave had kept me from throwing away. In my hurry to gather my things together that morning, I hadn't noticed which hat I was grabbing.

He understood right away. "Your lucky hat."

"Yup." I put it back on my head.

"Congratulations," Sam said, and we pushed off the lift. Neither of us spoke as we moved to the edge of the slope. I took a deep breath, and then I went over.

CHAPTER 20

APRIL

Sam Choi

Waiting for an interview with the bishop makes me feel like I've been called to the principal's office. I hate sitting there on display for anyone who walks by. I just know they are all doing the math in their heads to see why you're there. ("Hmmm, when is Sam Choi's birthday? Is it coming up? Why else would he be there? Unless he has some huge sin to confess.")

Okay, I admit that sounds paranoid.

There are some definite similarities, though. You trade reassurances with the other people sitting there waiting, like you do when you're waiting for the principal.

"What are you waiting for?" the girl next to me asked, and I told her, "Mission interview."

She smiled. "I'm waiting to talk to him about getting a recommend to do baptisms for the dead."

Once we had that covered, we both sat there waiting for our summons. The bishop was running late, just like the principal.

I guess this sounds like I've been to the principal's office a million times. I've only been twice. Both times were in elementary school, and both times were with Cody. What we'd done wasn't that bad. (We couldn't seem to stop ourselves from sneaking fake barf under the door of the faculty bathroom.) But after the second time, our parents threatened us with our lives and well-being and other, more important things (like not being able to play Little League that summer). I guess we learned our lesson because we hadn't done anything like that since, although I knew Cody still had the fake barf. You'd think they would have known enough to take it away.

Anyway, there I was, sitting in the foyer of our church building, waiting for the bishop to open the door and invite me inside. The guy before me was taking a long time. I loosened my tie, then reconsidered and cinched it back up. I wasn't looking forward to the interview.

Bishop Landry used to be the scoutmaster. He'd been a good one. We'd had a lot of fun until I slacked off at the end, when snowboarding became a lot more important to me than doing those last few Eagle requirements. I really didn't want to tell him about my mission doubts. He'd already been disappointed in me before, although he'd never mentioned it.

But I'd told Addie that I would tell the bishop the truth.

• • •

On the last day of snowboarding, Addie and I had been riding up on the lift for one of our runs when it had stopped for awhile. I didn't mind being stuck. I wondered if Addie did. We hung up there in the sky, suspended in the warmer March air, swinging our feet and looking down at everything and everyone. The world below us was blue and green and gray and white—the sky, the trees, the snow, a few rocks peeking out. It was so warm that I hadn't even put on my hat, and the wind ruffled my hair. If I went on a mission, I would miss this.

I said so to Addie, only I left out the "if" and used "when."

"When do you have your interview with the bishop?" she asked.

"Tuesday."

"That's cool. Are you excited?"

"No."

"Oh."

I was sick of hiding how I felt from everyone. And Addie had confided in me about liking Rob, so I figured it was okay if I told her the truth about how I felt about serving a mission. Besides, who else could I talk to? Rob and Cody weren't going on missions. They were cool with it, but it's not like they understood what it was all about. "I think it'd be cool to live in another country," Rob had told me, and I didn't know how to explain to him that it wasn't like going on a two-year study abroad program. But Addie knew all about missions. All of her brothers had gone on missions, except for Eric, who wasn't nineteen yet.

"I don't know if I want to go on a mission," I said to Addie.

"I just assumed—"

"Everyone just assumes." It sounded more bitter than I'd meant. "Sorry. I'm not mad at you."

"That's okay." She paused. "Why don't you want to go?"

"I think I might be too much of a wimp."

"What makes you say that? You're not a wimp at all."

I cleared my throat. "One time, at the beginning of last year, I went to a party with Rob and Cody. People were drinking. Someone offered me something." I stopped. I looked at Addie's face, waiting for disgust to show, but all I saw was surprise.

"What happened?"

"I took it. I drank it. I only thought about it for a second, and then I went ahead and did it. Cody and Rob didn't see me. I don't think the kid who gave it to me even remembers it happened. Maybe no one even knows. But I know."

I took a deep breath and went on. "I knew it was wrong, and I still did it. And this was at a party in my hometown, Addie. If I'm weak in a situation like that, then I'm going to be a complete waste on a mission."

Addie was quiet for a minute. "But you haven't done it again." It was a statement, not a question.

"No, I haven't done it again."

"So you repented."

"Well, yeah. It took a few months, but I finally went in and talked to my old bishop about it and everything."

"Sam, you took care of it. You shouldn't beat yourself up over it."

"It doesn't change the fact that I was weak when it mattered."

"But you've been strong other times since, right?"

"I guess. After that time I didn't want to do it again. It wasn't worth it."

"You know my sister-in-law—Avery? She had some trouble with Word of Wisdom stuff too. And look at her now."

"But I bet all of that was before she was baptized, right?" Addie's silence told me the answer. "See? It doesn't count. She wasn't even Mormon yet."

"Sam, plenty of people have made mistakes. Everyone has weaknesses. You just don't know about all the mistakes other people make."

"I just don't know what I'm going to do. I can't even tell my parents how I feel. The way I'm going, I'll end up telling them when I get my call."

Addie looked at me, and I knew what she was going to say, so I said it first. "I know, I know. I need to take care of it before then."

"You should tell the bishop you're not sure about this. I bet he'll have some ideas."

"Yeah, but then I'll have to do something about it." I tried to laugh.

Addie didn't laugh. "It must be hard to be a guy and know that everyone expects a mission out of you. I hate living up to other people's expectations."

The lift started up again. We both were silent until we were nearing the top. Addie handed me the star-spangled beanie as we got off the lift. "I think you're going to need this."

"Why?" I thought she was talking about the interview with the bishop, and I pictured myself walking into his office wearing that hat.

Instead, she said, "Because we're going to race down this time, and you'll need all the luck you can get." She took off, and I had to hurry and put on the hat and try to catch her. The hat *was* lucky too, because I beat her.

Although, maybe she had meant to give me luck for more than just the run down the hill, because at the end of the day, she didn't ask for her hat back. And I didn't offer.

. . .

Bishop Landry finally opened the door. An older man in our ward walked out of the office. "Come on in, Sam." Bishop Landry smiled at me and held out his hand. I shook it and walked through the door.

I looked around as I sat down in the chair in front of the bishop's desk. I hadn't been in there since my last big confession, with the old bishop. The office looked basically the same.

Bishop Landry asked, "Is there anything you want to talk about before we get started?"

"No," I said. Weak. Weak.

I answered all the questions exactly right. I obeyed the Word of Wisdom, was morally clean, paid my tithing, everything.

Bishop Landry asked if there was anything in my past that should have been resolved but hadn't.

"No," I said. "I mean, there was, but I talked to Bishop Green, and—"

"If you've already talked with him and been through the repentance process, then I don't need to hear about it. Unless you want to talk about it, of course."

"You'd think less of me if I didn't go on a mission, right?" I blurted out.

Bishop Landry leaned across his desk and met my eyes. "I know you are a good kid, Sam. What you decide to do about a mission won't change my opinion of you."

"But you think I should go, don't you?"

"It doesn't matter what I think. This is your decision, and it's between you and the Lord. I'm here to guide and help you in making that decision if I can, but it's not my choice to make."

"I know." I paused. "Missionary work is hard for me. That sounds like a cop-out. But I honestly don't think I can do it. Tell other people what to believe, I mean. I don't think I can walk up to people, tell them to change their lives, and act like I have all the answers to everything."

"Tell me what you've been doing to get ready for your mission," Bishop Landry said.

"Well, I've been going on splits with the missionaries." I paused, thinking of that one experience. Should I call it a "split" since I'd only gone once? "And my parents are using the Preach My Gospel manual for family home evenings. So Alex and I are getting familiar with that."

"How's your personal scripture study?"

"Uh, it used to be pretty bad. I didn't do it very often. But I've been getting better the past couple of months, ever since I started worrying about this whole mission thing."

"And have you been getting any answers from your reading and studying?"

"Not that I can tell."

"Keep trying, Sam. If you put everything you can into it, you'll get an answer eventually."

"All right."

"Why don't we meet again in a couple of months and see how things are going?"

I agreed. The two of us shook hands, and then I went back out into the hall. The girl was sitting patiently waiting her turn, and she and I both said, "See you" as she went in to talk to the bishop. The door closed behind them, and I started walking down the hall.

I had to laugh. *Keep trying?* What kind of advice was that?

CHAPTER 21

APRIL

Caterina Giovanni

It was the end of the semester, and I'd been saying good-byes all week. Noelle, Liz, Chase, Brett, everyone in our ward . . . the exodus started at the beginning of finals week and kept on going.

I was the last to leave our apartment. Jenna, of course, was already gone, and Noelle and Liz packed up together and left as soon as they had finished their finals. As usual, I somehow managed to have one of the last finals scheduled, so I had to stay until the bitter end of the semester. And it *was* bitter. The weather was extra cold, and I had to wear my winter parka all week long.

I hated saying good-bye, and I was even more convinced now that I'd rather be the one to go first. I was glad I had the job in Seattle lined up. I wasn't quite ready to go home, but I didn't want to stay in Rexburg without Noelle and Liz.

After I finished my last test, I walked across campus alone. Rexburg was emptying out. Places that had been packed with people were vacant and still, and the campus felt like a ghost town. I felt a little transparent myself as I walked home to pack. I didn't see anyone I knew the whole way there.

• • •

I picked the stars off, one by one, from the ceiling of the room I'd shared with Jenna. At first, taking them down seemed all sad and poignant and symbolic. Before too long, though, my neck started to kill from leaning back to pull them down and it got boring; I was annoyed and just wanted the job to be over with as quickly as possible.

Late that night, I took the stickers out to the dumpster. A few of them escaped and blew away in the dark, still glowing, and I felt sad. They reminded me of the summer fireflies at home in Ithaca, and of course, they reminded me of Jenna.

• • •

After the isolation of my last couple of days in Rexburg, I liked being part of a group of people again. Andrea's mom and ten-year-old sister, Chloe, picked me up at the Sea-Tac Airport. They were friendly and made me feel comfortable right away. That night, a man named Paul came over for dinner. I remembered Andrea telling me about him. I knew he and Sister Beckett had been dating for a long time, and it was obvious that they were getting serious.

I guess college students don't have a monopoly on romance.

It didn't take long before I fell into a routine. Sister Beckett invited me to come to the institute class she taught. It was a missionary prep class, which I wouldn't need for awhile, but I figured I might as well go. Especially if she was as good a teacher as her daughter had been.

I hit it off with one guy in my class right away. His name was Sam Choi, and he was going on a mission in the fall. He was funny and cute and easy to talk to, and he knew the Becketts. His sister had married Andrea's brother in February.

My job started three days after I got to Seattle. In the mornings, I woke up and rode the bus into the city to work. Once I was there,

I spent a lot of time interviewing patients about their care and then compiling statistics on a computer for the research project I'd been assigned. I'd thought the research might be depressing. In some ways it was because I was talking with patients who were going through a lot, but it was also inspiring.

Plus, I felt like I was doing something worthwhile with my time, which was refreshing after two semesters of college. I'd liked my classes and everything, but it was fulfilling to get back into the real world for a change. I ate lunch at the research center with my other coworkers, and we talked about how the project was going. It felt grown up.

After work, I rode the bus home and helped Sister Beckett with dinner. On the nights I didn't have my institute class, I would read, or watch TV, or hang out with Chloe. I felt a lot of empathy for her as the youngest in a family with everyone else gone. She and I played a lot of games and watched a lot of movies.

One night, we were watching the Steve Martin version of *Father of the Bride*. "I wonder when Paul is going to ask my mom to marry him," Chloe said matter-of-factly during the scene where the daughter announces her engagement.

I turned to look at her in surprise. She kept talking. "I think he wanted to ask her at Christmas, but then he found out Ethan was going to ask Mikey, and he decided to wait."

"Really?" I asked. "Did he tell you that?"

"Sort of. Right before Christmas, my mom had this big talk with me about how she might marry Paul, and she wanted to know how I would feel about it. I told her I would be happy about it. And then Paul asked me if I knew what my mom's favorite color was because she wouldn't tell him. I think he wanted to get her something different for her ring because she's already had a diamond."

"Did you tell him?" It would be so weird to be ten years old and having someone ask you what color of ring to buy your mom. Chloe didn't seem bothered by it, however.

"Yup. I told him her favorite color is blue. But then we found out that Ethan was going to propose to Mikey over the Christmas break, and Paul didn't ask my mom to marry him after all. Andrea and I thought he might ask her on Valentine's Day, but he didn't. We think it's because it was right when Ethan's wedding was happening."

"Wow. That's exciting."

Chloe shrugged. "I already have a dad. But it would be nice for Mom to have someone too, since she doesn't have Dad anymore."

•   •   •

After Chloe and I finished our movie, I took my laptop outside to sit on the front porch and check my e-mail. I liked the evenings in Washington. Even though Seattle was across the country from New York, the weight of the water in the air at night reminded me of Ithaca. But I still hadn't seen any fireflies.

I opened my laptop, and when the monitor lit up, a moth flew right into it and then blundered away, startled. It made me laugh. I waited for my e-mail to appear on the screen. I was hoping to hear from Steve and some other friends at home.

Where *was* home these days? When I had visited Ithaca at Christmastime, I felt like it was still where I was from, but I wasn't sure it was where I was going. Seattle was fine, but I felt like a more-knowledgeable-than-usual tourist on an extended vacation. Rexburg was familiar, but I didn't know that I would ever think of it as "home." I knew my stay there was temporary, lasting only as long as I went to school at BYU–Idaho. I wondered, not for the first time, where I would end up and where my home would be eventually.

Obviously you can tell I never moved around much as a kid. Here I was feeling all displaced after less than a year on my own. I was also feeling lonely and uncertain about myself, a feeling I *hated.* The last few months had taught me that I didn't have all the answers, that I couldn't solve everyone's problems, and that sometimes I couldn't even solve my own. How did I feel about Steve? Was I a good friend and roommate? Had we helped Jenna at all, or had we made things even worse for her? My first semester of college had been an exciting, crazy ride. My second semester had been about growing up, and I couldn't tell if I'd done a very good job.

There was an e-mail from Jenna in my inbox. She'd written only once before. That had been a short e-mail, and she sent the same one to Liz and Noelle and me. All she said was that she had gotten home safely, and she appreciated everything we'd done for her. We'd all written back, but that had been almost a month ago, and none of us knew what had happened since. I started to read.

Hey Cate, what's up? Things are going pretty well. My parents finally got me to try some counseling to help with some of the issues I keep having trouble with. It makes me feel like a freak. I hate that I'm the kind of person who has issues, but the counseling seems to be helping.

I think I hit rock bottom the day I came home from Rexburg. I walked back into my room and felt like "Here I am again, right back in the same place I was at this time last year." I cried and cried. I felt like I hadn't gotten anywhere. That nothing had changed.

It's sort of strange that I had a prompting when I didn't deserve to have one. I think it was because of my parents', not my own, worthiness. Whatever the reason, I think it's turned out to be a good thing that I came home. I'm still hoping to be back in the fall.

Well, enough about me. Sorry about that. How is everything going in Washington? Are you excited to be there? Is the family you're living with nice? Is the job working out?

I wrote Jenna back. *I'm glad to hear from you. I'm liking Seattle a lot.* I told her about my job and about living with the Becketts.

I also told her, *Don't worry about having issues. We all have issues. At least you're trying to take care of yours.*

CHAPTER 22

APRIL

Addie Sherman

I sat across the kitchen table from Avery, writing furiously on my assignment sheet while she talked. "Slow down! I can't keep up with you!"

Avery paused. "Sorry." I tried to write down the cascade of words she'd been sending my way, but I was sure I'd missed some of it. She was helping me with a question about symbolism. There's nothing I hate more than symbolism.

Since the last snowboarding trip, I'd gotten in the habit again of going over to Dave and Avery's to hang out with Avery. Now we worked on my English homework almost every time I was there. Avery said it was payback for all the times I'd helped her with stuff for the reunion.

"You definitely love English," I complained to Avery as I finished writing.

"I know. But it wasn't always that way. I didn't start to like it until I got to high school."

"What happened?"

"I had a teacher who changed everything. He made a really big difference in my life because he made me realize I loved writing. Then, when I started to figure out that reading and finding out more about the other parts of English enriched my writing, I was hooked on all of it."

"Even the symbolism?" I grumbled.

"Even the symbolism."

"So who was the teacher?"

"Mr. Thomas. But he retired."

"Hey!" I said. "That's who I have right now. He took over for Mrs. Bryant during her maternity leave."

"Are you serious?" Avery got all excited. "That's great, Addie! Don't you love him? Isn't he a great teacher?"

"He's the best English teacher I've had so far." I was doing better with his assignments than I ever had with Mrs. Bryant's, so he was fine in my book. Plus, he was very kind and very real.

Avery couldn't get over it. "I haven't seen him in forever. He came to our wedding reception, which was so nice of him. He must get invited to a million of those a year. And for our wedding gift, he gave us a subscription to *The New Yorker*. It was so thoughtful. He knows I love writing, and they have great short stories." She started to laugh. "He also gave us a framed photograph of the school mascot."

"I don't get it."

"Dave and I accidentally destroyed the school mascot when he was a senior and I was a junior."

"Oh, boy." That didn't surprise me. Dave can be destructive even when he doesn't mean to be.

"Anyway, will you tell him hello for me?"

I promised that I would.

"I heard a rumor that he was joining the Church, but I never heard if he did."

"If he did, he must not live in our stake," I said.

"We'd all know by now," she agreed. "That's so cool that Mr. Thomas is teaching again."

A few minutes later, we had finished with my assignment. I packed all my books and notes away in my bag and looked at Avery. "What do you want to do next?"

"I have a couple of errands to run out in Lynnwood. Should we go for a drive?"

I wasn't surprised. Avery seemed to want to go for a drive every time I came over. She always had an errand to do, but I got the idea it was the driving part she liked, not the getting-things-done part. She liked to ride in the passenger seat and look out the window because it was uncomfortable for her to sit behind the wheel these days. We usually took her car. It was much more dependable than mine.

"I feel like everything has changed," she said, looking out the window at a new housing development that was going up. Evergreen trees lay like fallen soldiers, their torn roots reaching out for earth and ground and life. "It's a whole new season. Things don't look the same. It's like the last few months passed me by."

I knew what she was talking about. I've had that feeling of detachment before, of getting by. In fact, I'd had it for a long time. It seemed like it had only been during the past few months that I'd emerged into the real world again.

I flipped the wipers on to skim away the raindrops that had started to fall.

"I've been wanting to ask you," I said. "What did you say to my mom last week to convince her to let me go snowboarding?"

"I called her and told her it was partly my fault you'd had trouble in English. I told her I hadn't made it easy for you to ask for help because I was always needing help instead."

"Oh." I didn't know what to say. It was partly true, after all.

"I said I felt guilty, and that I wanted to be able to pay you back for all the help you'd given me. Then I told her I knew it was none of my business, but there was only one weekend left to snowboard, and I wished you could go."

"And it worked. She let me go."

"How was the snowboarding anyway?"

"The weather was warm and the snow terrible, but otherwise it was perfect." I turned off the freeway. "Thanks for talking to her."

"No problem. I owed you."

"You've more than made up for it." It made me uncomfortable sometimes when Avery talked about how much she owed all of us for helping her through the past few months. I was worried she was keeping a scorecard in her mind and that she wouldn't be able to rest until she made things even.

"Do you go to seminary?" she asked me out of the blue.

"Not always," I admitted. "I try to, but sometimes I don't make it out of bed in time." Then I felt a little defensive. "Why? You never went, right?"

"No. I never did. Sorry if that bugged you." Lately, Avery catches on when I'm ticked, and she doesn't pretend it's not happening. I like that about her. "I wasn't trying to get after you. I was just curious. I'm not exactly in a position to talk. Look at me, I was the world's biggest blob on bed rest. I haven't gone anywhere or done anything for months."

"You're going somewhere right now," I pointed out.

"But you're at the wheel. That's what's been freaking me out about this whole pregnancy thing. I'm not in control of any of it anymore. I do what I can, but it doesn't guarantee a single thing."

"Speaking of out of control," I said, "I'm going to pull over for a minute." The rain was coming down so hard that I couldn't see. I pulled into the parking lot of a shopping center.

Avery took a deep breath, which turned into a shudder. "I thought it was wrong to get depressed when you have the gospel in your life. But this has been hard." She wasn't crying, but it looked a lot harder than crying would be.

"You should go ahead and cry," I said awkwardly. "You've had a rough couple of months."

Avery took my advice as the rain pounded around us. I couldn't tell if there were other cars parked near us, or if we were marooned on the black asphalt sea. I didn't turn off the wipers or hug Avery. I didn't know how to stop either flood from happening.

Avery looked so small, I reached over and patted her arm. She grabbed my hand and held onto it and kept crying.

The two of us were struggling along together. We had been for months, but I hadn't recognized it until recently. Our situations were totally different, but we were keeping each other company through it all.

I do have something in common with someone in my family.

CHAPTER 23

MAY

Sam Choi

"This is going to be great," Mikey told Alex and me the day she and Ethan moved back to Seattle for the summer. "You and Ethan will have a chance to get to know each other better. You can be *brothers*." She had to know how cheesy that sounded, but she said it anyway.

I rolled my eyes. Alex was worse. *"Brother,"* he said in a dramatic, deep voice as he reached out to hug Ethan. Everyone started laughing.

Mikey and Ethan had decided to come to Seattle to work for the summer, since jobs pay better here. They were living with us because we had more space than either of Ethan's parents. Our house felt a lot more crowded with two additional people living in it. I wouldn't have thought it would make such a big difference.

It wasn't too bad having them around, though. Mikey was fun, and Ethan was quiet and didn't go all crazy trying to fit in. He was busy with his new job, and I was busy with school and AP tests and all of that. We were all getting along fine.

I guess we weren't bonding enough for Mikey, however, because one Saturday morning she pulled me aside and told me to hang out with Ethan while she and Mom were gone shopping. She'd tried to corner Alex, too, but Dad was taking him somewhere to get supplies for his Eagle Scout project.

Mikey must have told Ethan the same thing she'd told me, because after she left, he wandered into the family room where I was sitting and watching TV. He looked uncomfortable. It was like she had set us up on a brotherhood date. A man date. A man date that had been mandated by my sister. Ha. Not bad. I almost told Ethan my hilarious joke, but decided he would think I was weird.

"So . . . Alex is getting his Eagle?" he asked, trying to make conversation.

"It looks like it."

Like I said before, I'd never gotten my Eagle. Luckily, Dad hadn't ever gotten his, and he'd turned out okay, or so he had pointed out to Mom when she got after me about it. Alex, on the other hand, was totally into his project. There would be no stopping him.

Mom would be thrilled.

I looked out the window. It was raining hard outside, so we couldn't go out in the back and shoot hoops. We'd had a wet April, even for Seattle. I don't know why all that precipitation couldn't have happened back in March, so they wouldn't have closed Snoqualmie Pass early, but what can you do?

Anyway, we couldn't shoot hoops, and it didn't seem like either of us could figure out what else we should do. We were sitting there staring out the window, waiting for the rain to let up or for someone to come home. Awkwardness all over the place. I wondered if this was how Addie felt when she had started hanging out with her sister-in-law all the time. I had a whole new respect for her.

"What did you do for your Eagle project?" Ethan was still trying to make conversation.

"Nothing. I never got it."

"Oh."

I looked out the window for the fiftieth time to see if it had stopped raining yet. It hadn't, but it did seem to be letting up some. I could see Ethan trying to think of another topic. This was brutal.

His next choice was even worse than the Eagle questions. "So when are you turning in your mission papers?"

"I don't know. Never."

Ethan looked at me. He was surprised. I was, too. Why did I keep telling people the truth about this? First Addie, then the bishop, now Ethan. I kept talking even though I knew I should shut up. "I'm not sure I want to go."

"Why not?" He asked it like he was interested, not like he was shocked or disgusted.

So I answered him. "I don't know if it's for me. Everyone talks about what the ideal missionary is like and how perfect missions are. None of that sounds like me."

Ethan looked surprised. "Where did you get that idea?"

"What idea?"

"The one about missions being perfect."

"Well, yours was, wasn't it?" Just last night at dinner, he'd told us a story about celebrating his first Christmas in Brazil. Everyone had been mesmerized. Mom practically cried. She got all teary and kept looking over at me in this significant way. She probably wanted me to grab a pencil and start taking notes.

"I'm glad I went, but it wasn't easy all of the time. It wasn't easy *most* of the time."

"That's news to me," I said. "All the returned missionaries I know act like it was the best time they've ever had."

"It's some of both. The best *and* the worst. It was definitely one of the hardest times of my life. I got tired. I got discouraged." He paused. "There was one time when we had the font all filled up and all the people there for a baptism, and the guy didn't show. And he never wanted to talk to us again. Actually, that happened more than once. But the first time was the hardest."

"Yeah, but you made it through. Who knows if I would make it through stuff like that. I'd want to quit."

"You might want to quit, but you wouldn't."

"How do you know?" I hated it when people said things like that. They couldn't know that I wouldn't quit.

"You're right, I don't," Ethan said. "But I bet you would be a good missionary."

"Nothing like you." I decided to make some assumptions of my own, since Ethan thought he knew all about me. "I bet you were the guy that everyone looked up to, and all your companions thought you were a hero."

Ethan laughed. "Right. There was this one time when my companion told me he hated me and I was the worst person on the face of the planet. He said I didn't have a testimony, and everything I did was fake, like I was putting on a show. He meant it, too. That was one of the low points."

"How come no one mentions stuff like that in their talks when they get home?" I asked Ethan.

"I don't know. We should."

"I don't think I should go unless I believe in all of it. I shouldn't be trying to talk people into a religion unless I know it's true."

"I'm with you. You shouldn't go unless you believe what you're doing. You'll get tested enough out there."

"You're really selling it, Ethan," I told him. I couldn't help laughing.

He started laughing too. "Sorry. Should I tell you some of the cool parts too?"

"I think I've heard all of that before. No offense."

The rain had let up enough. "You want to go outside now?" I asked. "We can shoot around for awhile."

"Okay. I haven't played much since my mission, but I bet I can still waste you."

I looked at Ethan in surprise. "Oh, yeah? You're on."

• • •

"Did you guys have fun?" Mikey asked. She and Mom had arrived home to find Ethan and me playing one-on-one. We'd lowered the rim so we could dunk, which is a standard Choi playing rule. Alex and I are both of the opinion that if there isn't a chance we can dunk, what's the point of playing?

Mikey looked at the two of us and waited for an answer. She was probably trying to detect signs of bonding. I decided to humor her.

"We had *so* much fun." My voice oozed sincerity. "I *love* my new brother."

That cracked Ethan up, and he stopped paying attention, so I dunked on him.

The trash talk must have reassured Mikey that we were bonding, because she went inside. It was too bad she left when she did, because Alex arrived a few minutes later, and we took it to a whole new level.

CHAPTER 24

MAY

Caterina Giovanni

Romance was in the air. I could tell. I have a sixth sense about these kinds of things. If anyone is about to get engaged or fall in love, I know it even before they do.

Okay, I'm kidding. I don't really have a sixth sense at all. But there were a few obvious circumstances that seemed to indicate a proposal from Paul was going to take place in the near future.

First, all of the Beckett kids were in town, which was rare. Andrea and Joel had come to visit for a few weeks, to take a break after their finals and to go to a reunion that Andrea's friends were having. Mikey and Ethan were living over at the Chois for the summer.

Second, Paul took Andrea and Chloe shopping one night, and they came back with bright eyes, whispering a lot. Sister Beckett pretended not to notice.

Third, both Sister Beckett and Paul were acting extra happy. They were usually happy, but this seemed different.

And last, Paul came over Saturday afternoon and announced he had booked reservations for a fancy dinner cruise for that evening, and everyone was invited. Me included.

To be honest, I was dying to go. I wanted to see the proposal, and the dinner cruise sounded interesting (they have them in Ithaca, too, but I'd never been on one before). But, even though I wanted to be there, I had a feeling this was one time I should sit out.

So I said thanks a ton, but that I had plans. Then I went ahead and made some. I called Mikey's brother Sam from my missionary prep class and asked him on a date.

"Hey, Sam, this is Cate. You know, from institute?"

"Yeah, of course. What's up?"

"You know how the Becketts are having that big family dinner tonight?"

"Yeah, Mikey and Ethan are going. She thinks Paul is going to propose."

"That's what I think too. Anyway, they were polite and invited me, but I thought it would be better if it was just family. So I told them I had a date, which wasn't exactly true because I don't have one, but I'm trying to get one. Would you like to be it?"

Sam laughed. "Sure. I don't have any plans tonight."

"Perfect. Um, do you think you could drive? I don't have a car."

"No problem. Where are we going?"

"I don't know yet."

"Do you want some ideas?"

"Definitely. I still don't know my way around here all that well."

"There's a good restaurant down by the waterfront that isn't too expensive. And then we could walk around for awhile. They have live music at the pavilion most weekends."

"That sounds great."

"I can call a friend and we can double. If you want to."

"Sure."

• • •

Sam picked me up last. I climbed into the front seat of the car while he held the door open for me. The other couple was sitting in the backseat of his car. Sam introduced us: "Cate, this is Addie, and this is Rob. Addie and Rob, this is Cate. My date."

Everyone laughed at the rhyme, and the rest of the night every-one called me Cate the Date, which I didn't mind. It was fun to be around people who were basically my age again. Playing board games with Chloe was great, don't get me wrong, but the only date I'd had for awhile had been with Professor Plum or Colonel Mustard.

It didn't take too long to drive to the restaurant. We parked and walked down the street, which I liked very much because it reminded me of home. There was a Thai food place, an organic grocery store, a small store with expensive, hand-dyed clothing, places like that. It was like Ithaca, only more self-consciously trendy.

Once we were inside the restaurant, it only took me about five minutes to figure out that Sam liked Addie. It's possible I have a sixth sense after all. I'm not positive about what gave him away, since he was trying hard to be attentive to me, and he wasn't obviously flirting with her. I think it was the way he snapped to attention every time she spoke, and when she walked through the door he was holding open for all of us, he turned to watch her go. He also knew where she was at any given moment.

It made me feel a little sad. I mean, it's not like I had a big crush on Sam. He was cute, but I was leaving soon, and I'd only known him a few weeks. He was going on a mission, blah blah blah. (Plus, I admit I was focused on what it would be like to see Steve again in a few days.)

But talk to any girl in the world, and I bet she'll say the same thing: Noticing a guy noticing the girl he likes makes you wish some-one were noticing *you* like that.

Got that? It's true.

Anyway, Rob and Addie were friendly. They both thought it was cool I was from New York and asked me all kinds of questions. I'd met Addie briefly at church, but this was the first chance I'd had to talk to her, and I decided I liked her a lot. Dinner went by quickly, and soon we were stepping out of the restaurant and walking toward the waterfront.

It was a beautiful night, one of the warmest I'd experienced in Seattle. I wondered how things were going with the Becketts. I wondered what Paul's last name was. Would Andrea's mom change her name to his? Then her last name would be different from her kids. Could she hyphenate it? Did Paul have any children? I didn't think he did, but I hadn't asked.

Dating seems complicated enough when you're young. I can't imagine what it would be like if you were almost fifty, and divorced, and there were kids involved. That would be rough.

I hoped Paul would propose tonight. Sister Beckett deserved someone wonderful.

"What are you thinking about?" Sam asked me.

"Weddings," I told him. Sam looked like I'd surprised him, which I probably had. "You know, Sister Beckett's wedding. I wonder if Paul is proposing right now."

"What if you're wrong, and he just wanted to take them all out somewhere nice?"

"I guess I could be wrong," I said, but I knew I wasn't, and it must have shown in my voice or expression. Sam started to laugh.

We were getting close to the pavilion by the bay, and Sam started slowing down. "Do you want to get some ice cream?"

"Okay. What about them?" I gestured to Rob and Addie, who were still walking ahead of us.

"They'll figure it out." Sam opened the door for me, and a chime rang. It was the kind of laid-back store where the owner lets his dog sit out front; the dog looked lazily at us while we walked inside. I patted him on the head.

I didn't need very long to decide what I wanted. "Two scoops of Rocky Road," I told the kid behind the counter. I waited for Sam to order, and then I asked him, "So, are we trying to give Addie and Rob time alone?"

"That's the idea." He sounded sad. "Addie's had a crush on Rob forever, but he had a girlfriend until a couple of weeks ago. I think he's been wanting to ask Addie out, but he hadn't had a chance until tonight."

I laughed. "We're quite the unselfish couple. I put together this whole date so I could get out of the Becketts' way, and you saw it as a chance to nudge Rob to ask Addie out."

Sam nodded. "You're right. When we go on a date, everyone wins."

We had a little argument over who would pay for the ice cream cones (I won because Sam paid for dinner even though I'd asked him out). We stepped back outside and sat on a bench in the shade.

"So how long have *you* liked Addie?"

Sam turned to me in shock and then started to laugh. "Wow, is it that obvious? That's embarrassing."

"It's not *that* obvious. Only a perceptive, awesome girl would notice."

Sam smiled. "That does describe you." Then he looked worried. "Do you think *she's* noticed?"

"I don't know." I didn't. It all depended on how she felt about Rob. If she wasn't interested in Rob, she might have noticed how Sam was acting. But if she *was* interested, she wouldn't have noticed and wouldn't care. She would be focused on Rob.

I kept my thoughts to myself. I didn't think Sam would like either answer, no matter how unselfish he was trying to be.

• • •

After we'd finished our ice cream, we met back up with Rob and Addie. The four of us sat on some of the larger rocks in the bay and hung our feet into the water. We watched people and birds and boats and talked and laughed with the music of the bluegrass band that was playing in the background. It was a nice night. I tried to watch Addie and Rob without being completely transparent about it. They were obviously good friends, but so were she and Sam. I thought Sam still had a chance.

Sam drove me home last. He opened the door for me, and we started up the sidewalk.

"It doesn't look like the Becketts are back yet," he said. The porch light was on, but the house was very quiet, and the cars were missing from the driveway.

"They must still be out celebrating." We stopped under the porch light, and I pulled my house key out of my pocket. "Thanks for going tonight."

"I'm glad you called, Cate. I had a good time."

"Me too. And thanks for driving and dinner and everything."

"I was glad to do it."

"You're a good sport, Sam."

"You too. Thanks for listening to me gripe about Addie."

"No problem."

"I'll see you at institute, right?" Sam asked as he turned to leave.

"Yup. I'm not leaving for another week or two. I'll be there."

"Great." Sam waved and started down the steps. Before he got to his car, I called out to him.

"Sam? You can tell me to mind my own business, but I don't think you should give up."

He pretended not to know what I was talking about. "Give up on what?"

"On Addie. If you like her, you should do something about it. You'll regret it later if you don't."

CHAPTER 25

MAY

Addie Sherman

The morning after my date with Rob, I went straight to Avery's house. I had to talk to someone. I thought I'd ask Avery if she wanted to go for a drive, and maybe I could bring up what had happened and how I was feeling. I hadn't been able to sleep much after Rob and Sam had dropped me off. Even when I'd fallen asleep, I'd kept replaying parts of the night over and over in my dreams.

Dave's car wasn't in the driveway—he must have gone to work early or was out running errands—but someone else's car was there. It looked familiar, but I couldn't quite place it. I ran up the steps and rang the doorbell even though Avery had told me a million times to walk right in.

Sam's older sister, Mikey, answered it. Great. She was the one visiting Avery. No wonder the car looked familiar. Now how was I going to talk to Avery about Rob and Sam? There was no way I could do that in front of Sam's sister. Mikey is nice, though, so I tried to sound like I was happy to see her.

"Oh, hey, Mikey."

"Hi, Addie. Come in. I'm helping Avery out with the reunion stuff."

"Oh, that's nice of you," I said lamely. I followed Mikey down the hall toward the kitchen.

Avery was sitting at the table, which was covered in lists and papers.

"You guys have been busy," I said.

"Now that I'm here, I can actually help. I feel bad Avery has been doing everything so far." Mikey sat down at the table.

"Addie's been helping too," Avery said.

"Oh, just with the invitations, mostly." The three of us looked at each other and started laughing, remembering the misspelling.

Mikey consulted one of the lists. "We're almost done here. In fact, the only thing left to do is find a bagpiper."

"A bagpiper?" I looked at Avery.

"It's not my idea," she said. "This one is all Mikey. She wants to have something authentically Scottish."

"I thought of haggis first," Mikey said. I must have looked blank, because she went on. "It's this famous Scottish dish that's made from a lot of weird stuff like animal stomach. Once I looked into making it, I decided it was too disgusting. And Ethan and Dave flat-out refused to wear kilts. The only other Scottish thing I could think of was bagpipe music, so I want to find someone who plays the bag-pipes."

"You could buy a CD," I suggested.

"That's what I've been saying," Avery agreed.

Mikey reached under the table for her flip-flops. "Two against one. All right. I'll go buy a CD right now while I'm thinking about it. Is there anything else I should get while I'm out? I can order the balloons too."

"I think that's all we have to do. Andrea's in charge of setting up the sound system and finding the other, non-Scottish music. We've assigned out all the food. . . . We should be set." Avery leaned back in her chair a little. She looked uncomfortable, and big. She was getting closer and closer to her due date. I hoped she didn't have the baby the day of the reunion—it would be sad if she missed it after all her hard work.

"All right. Call me if you think of anything else while I'm gone." Mikey slung her bag over her shoulder, slipped on her flip-flops, and headed out of the room.

I didn't waste any time after I heard the door close behind her. She'd be back soon, and I had to talk to Avery before then. "I went on a date last night," I blurted out.

Avery is the best. She didn't squeal or say, "Ooooh," or act like it was a freakish occurrence that I, Addie Sherman, had been asked on a date. She just smiled and said, "Tell me all about it."

So I did.

· · ·

The night before, I was in the middle of filling out applications for summer jobs when my mom brought me the phone. "It's Rob," she told me, handing it over. I wished for the millionth time that I had a cell phone so she wouldn't know each and every time any of my friends called.

"Hi, Rob," I said, putting the lifeguarding application on top of the stack. "What's up?"

"Not much. Hey, do you want to go out tonight?"

"Okay." I figured he and Sam and Cody must have planned something, and I didn't mind taking a break from trying to find gainful employment. "Where should I meet you guys?"

There was silence. "Um, I meant *out*, like on a date."

It was my turn to be speechless. I don't know how a whole bunch of thoughts managed to crowd into my head in the few seconds it took to answer him, but they did. *Rob and Brook broke up only two weeks ago. Why is Rob asking me out? If I go, will Brook be mad? Will*

Sam think that I like Rob? Do I still like Rob? Or do I like Sam? I thought I was over Rob . . . so why is my heart beating so fast?

The silence must have been bugging Rob, because he started talking again. "Sam is going too, and bringing this girl from his church class. He's the one who suggested I call you." Rob must have realized how that sounded. "I mean, I wanted to call you anyway, and then Sam mentioned it . . ." He sounded as awkward as I felt.

"It sounds fun. I'd love to go," I managed to say, realizing it was the truth.

"Okay, good. Sam and I will pick you up tonight around six. We're all going to ride together."

"I'll be ready. Thanks, Rob."

He and Sam were *both* going to pick me up? It was getting worse and worse. I hung up the phone and realized I had no clue who Sam's date was. A girl from his church class? Rob had to be talking about the missionary prep class that Sam was taking at institute. Had Sam met a college girl there?

Remind me again why you thought this would be fun? I asked myself.

Sam's date turned out to be Cate Giovanni, a girl who was living with the Becketts for a couple of months while she worked in Seattle. I'd met her at church before; she'd come with the Becketts, who're in my ward. Cate was cute and athletic and friendly, with long blonde hair. She and Sam were laughing like old friends as they walked back to the car and got inside.

But she and Sam *weren't* old friends. *I* was Sam's old friend. *Calm down,* I told myself. *Remember how you freaked out about Brook, and she turned out to be nice?* It turned out to be the same way with Cate. She was very different from Brook, but it was still impossible to dislike her. As the four of us talked during dinner, Cate seemed like she was pretty cool too. Great. Why couldn't the guys like girls who were easy to hate?

After dinner, we walked along the waterfront. Somehow, Rob and I got ahead of Cate and Sam. I looked back but couldn't see them anywhere. Rob and I were making small talk as we wandered over the rocky beach near the pavilion where a bluegrass band was playing.

"Where's Cody tonight?" I asked.

"He had to work." Cody had already started his summer job working at one of those pizza places for little kids. He had to dress up as a giant bunny and wander around while the kids screamed and ran around and got pizza on his costume. The weekend before, some teenage kid thought it would be funny to trip Cody as he walked past. Cody had stood up and yelled at the kid in his non-bunny voice and let the kid know that the next time he did that, Cody would pound him. Now the manager was keeping a close eye on Cody and had been giving him all the worst shifts.

"Poor Cody."

"Yeah," Rob agreed.

It was quiet again. Rob and I stood there without a single thing to say as the water lapped up against the rocks. A green glass bottle washed up on the shore. I bent down and looked inside the bottle, hoping there was a message, but it was just litter. "I'm going to throw this away," I told Rob and walked over to the nearest trash can. I looked back along the sidewalk, but there was still no sign of Sam and Cate.

I went back to where Rob was standing and gave him a little shove. "Hey. Why is this so awkward?"

He started laughing. "I don't know. Because it's a date?"

"I think there's more to it than that," I said. "You're not over Brook, are you?"

Rob looked embarrassed and tossed a rock into the bay. "I guess not." He looked at me with his huge brown eyes. "I thought I was, but it's still weird to be going out without her."

"Why'd you guys break up, anyway?" I hadn't really talked to him or Brook about their breakup. I didn't want them to think I was trying to butt into their personal lives.

"She feels like she's too young to have a steady boyfriend. She said we shouldn't be so exclusive and we should date other people too." Rob threw another rock into the bay, this one with more force. "That made me mad, so I told her if that was how she felt, maybe we should *only* date other people. So that's how it ended."

"No offense, Rob, but that was really stupid."

"I know."

"You should call her."

"I know. But there are other people I'm interested in too." Rob looked right at me.

"Oh, really?" I'm horrible at flirting. Absolutely horrible. I didn't know what else to say, so I was glad when I turned around and saw Sam and Cate walking toward us.

Rob followed my gaze. "Hey, where have you two been?"

I tried my best not to look too interested in the answer.

"We were getting some ice cream," Cate said. She and Sam joined us at the water's edge. Sam smiled at me and said something— I don't remember what it was, but I remember wishing at that moment (and for the rest of the night) that I was out with Sam, not Rob.

Yes, Rob was still cute, and yes, it was flattering that he liked me, but Sam was the one who mattered to me now. I wanted to be the one he sat next to, and the one he snuck off to eat ice cream with, and the one he drove home at the end of the night.

Instead, we were out on a double date with different people. Sam had done his best to line up Rob and me, probably to help us out because he thought I still liked Rob. And now Sam was with Cate, who was fun and who was in college, where Sam would be soon. Why would he want to hang out with a girl who was still in high school and who hadn't been smart enough to know a good guy when she saw one?

Could I have messed things up any more?

• • •

I asked Avery that question as I finished telling her about the date.

Her answer surprised me. "Of course you could have. You could have done something *much* worse."

"Like what?"

"You could have written a note declaring your undying love for Sam and then given it to him even though you knew he had a girlfriend. Then you could have spent months feeling stupid about it because he acted like it never happened." She smiled at me. "I'm speaking from personal experience, in case you can't tell."

"*You* did that? When you were in high school?" Once again, I was surprised by Avery. Writing a note like that seemed completely out of character for her. "Who was the guy?"

"It was your brother. And I told him that I liked him in his yearbook. *After* he started dating Andrea Beckett. It kind of freaked him out, so he pretended it never happened, and we never talked about it until after he got back from his mission."

I didn't know what to say. She had written a love note to Dave in his *yearbook?*

"Pretty bad, isn't it?" Avery asked. "I still get embarrassed for myself when I think about it."

"Well, yeah, but everything turned out fine between the two of you." I had to admire how gutsy Avery had been.

"It did, and I wouldn't be surprised if things sorted themselves out eventually with you and Rob and Sam. What I'm trying to tell you is that it's hard to figure out how relationships and people work. You haven't made any more mistakes than anyone else."

CHAPTER 26

JUNE

Sam Choi

"How do I keep getting roped into helping with all your parties?" I grumbled to Mikey.

"What are you talking about?" she asked. "This is the first party you've ever helped with."

I lifted the huge cooler out of the trunk of her car. "How quickly you forget. I wish *I* could forget. My fingers are still numb from tying bows on your stupid bubbles."

"Oh, I get it. You're still whining about the wedding reception," Mikey teased.

"Remind me again where Ethan is? What easy job did you give him while I do all the heavy lifting?"

"He's picking up the balloons."

I laughed. "That really *is* an easy job."

Mikey pretended to ignore me and gestured to one of the wooden picnic tables. "Can you slide that over here a little?"

"Of course." I shoved the picnic table in her direction. She yelped and jumped out of the way, although it wasn't even close to hitting her.

"Overwhelmed by my superhuman strength yet again." I shook my head. "You'd think you'd be prepared after all this time."

After a few minutes of shifting picnic tables around according to Mikey's specifications, we seemed to be finished. Mikey looked at her watch. "Where *is* Ethan?"

I didn't really think she expected an answer. "Is there anything else you want me to do?" I'd ridden my bike down to the waterfront park to help her out, and I wanted to clear out before the reunion actually got going.

Mikey was staring off into space, not answering. I followed her gaze. A small, brown-haired girl who had just climbed out of a car was coming our way. I recognized the girl right away from the graceful way she walked. It was Julie, the guest of honor for the reunion party. Mikey had seen Julie since she'd returned home from her mission, but I hadn't yet.

"Julie! You're not supposed to be here yet!" Mikey attacked Julie with a hug. "You're supposed to come later and make a big entrance!"

Julie smiled. "I know, but you know I've never liked that kind of thing. I thought I could come and help set up."

"You can't help! This is your party! Plus, I don't want you to see any of the surprises."

A horn honked, and Dave and Avery pulled into the parking lot. They had a lot to carry, and Avery was hugely pregnant, so Mikey ran off to help them. She called back to us over her shoulder. "Talk to Julie, Sam. Distract her! Don't let her do any work. Make her go behind the pavilion so she doesn't see anything!"

I saluted my sister, and Julie laughed. We walked around the side of the pavilion and found a wooden bench to sit on. "This should work," I said, sitting down next to Julie. She'd always been my favorite of Mikey's friends. Even in high school, she'd never been all shrieky like other girls could be, and she was a really good listener. She always wanted to find out about you, but not in a nosy way. Plus, she never treated me like a stupid kid even when I was one.

"Sam, how are you?" she asked, giving me a hug.

"I'm boring. You're the one who's been in Scotland. How was it?" I knew that was a generic way to ask about her entire mission, but I also knew she wouldn't hold it against me.

"It was . . ." She hunted for words. "It was everything."

I raised my eyebrows at her. "Everything?"

She laughed. "That's a bit vague, isn't it?" She had a little bit of a Scottish accent. Just enough to be cute, but not so much that it seemed contrived.

Julie went on. "It was hard, beautiful, funny, exhilarating, exhausting . . ." She laughed. "Is that enough adjectives for you? Or would you prefer the 'best eighteen months of my life' answer?"

"I like the first answer." And I really did. I thought about it for a minute as car doors slammed and people started arriving. They hadn't noticed Julie and me yet, and I was glad. I wanted to find out more.

"So your parents came to pick you up, right?"

"They did." The accent again. Guys were going to go crazy over it.

"Can I ask how that went?" Julie's parents weren't members of the Church, and at first, they'd been against her joining. They'd also had a hard time initially with the idea of her serving a mission. But they were good people, and they always supported her in the end.

"They were so impressed that they begged to be baptized while we were still in Scotland." Julie grinned to show me she was kidding. "I think that's what I was secretly hoping would happen, but it didn't. That's all right, though. If there's one thing I learned on my mission, it's that you can't force a true conversion, and that's the only kind worth having."

"Are you still glad they came?"

"Oh, absolutely. I loved showing them around and having them meet the mission president, and the other missionaries, and the members there. It would have been worth it for our last day alone."

"What happened?"

"I took them to my favorite spot in Scotland. There's a place called Holyrood Park, which is this little piece of highland wilderness right in the middle of the city. If you climb the tallest hill there, Arthur's Seat, you can see for miles. One of my companions and I used to take our scriptures up there and read them. Sometimes it was so beautiful that we just sat there and looked out at the view. I wanted my parents to see it at sunrise, so I took them up there early in the morning." Julie paused. "Have you ever been to Scotland, Sam?"

"No." I felt like saying, *I haven't been anywhere. I haven't done anything.* Suddenly, I wanted to go to new places and see new things. Was that enough reason to go on a mission?

"It's beautiful, especially Edinburgh. The morning I took my parents to the park, the gray stone spires were so beautiful and the view was clear enough that we could see all the way out to the water. The sun was hitting the grass and turned it bright green and gold."

"It sounds like Seattle," I said. Julie looked at me, surprised. I hurried to explain. "The colors do, anyway. You know. Gray and blue and green and gold." I waved my arm out at the water in the bay. The sun was behind a cloud, so there wasn't much gold, but the rest of it was there.

"You're right." Julie looked out at the bay for a few moments. "They are a little the same."

"Anyway," I said, feeling stupid. "You were standing there with your parents . . ."

"And there we were, standing at the top of a hill in Scotland together, and I felt the Spirit so strongly." Julie had tears in her eyes, but that was all right. Unlike guys, girls can cry in public and get away with it without totally shaming themselves.

"Did they feel it too?" I asked.

"I asked my mom later what she was thinking, and she said that she was thinking she felt like she was a part of something bigger. My stepdad agreed." She smiled. "Whatever different names we call it, we were there at the same time on that hill in Scotland, experiencing it together. When I think of how far we had to come to have that, it almost feels greedy to want anything more."

She was quiet for a second after she finished talking, and then someone called Julie's name.

We both turned to see who it was. A tall guy was walking toward us and waving at Julie.

"Oh," she said, sounding surprised but excited, and she stood up suddenly.

I knew who the guy was, even though I hadn't seen him in years. It was Tyler Cruz, the high school basketball star who'd gone to Lakeview High at the same time Mikey and Julie had. When we were younger, Alex and I used to pretend we were Tyler. We loved going to the high school basketball games and watching him dunk. No other high school player we knew could do that.

"It looks like the party's about to start," I said. "I should get out of here." Now that Tyler was closer, I could see he had a huge smile on his face.

Julie looked at me. "You're not staying?"

"Nah. This is for you and your friends. I'll see you soon, right? I want to hear more about your mission."

"I'm sure I'll be hanging around your house a lot, since Mikey's here for the summer."

I waved to Julie and headed over to the bike rack. After I'd unlocked my bike, I looked back. Tyler was towering over Julie and grinning at her, saying something that made her laugh. His arms hung awkwardly at his sides.

"You can hug her, buddy," I muttered to myself, and right then he did. I smiled and turned away.

I thought about what I'd almost said to Julie. *I haven't been anywhere. I haven't seen anything.* It wasn't totally true. I'd been a few places and seen a few things. But talking to Julie made me realize how much more was out there.

At the top of the hill, I looked back at the reunion in progress. Tyler and Julie were walking toward Dave and Avery. Ethan had finally arrived with the balloons, and Mikey kissed him as she reached out to help him with them. Two of the balloons, a blue one and a green one, escaped into the sky, and I heard my sister laugh. Andrea and her husband were setting up the music; I heard the squawk of a bagpipe before Andrea hurried to turn the CD player off. A few other people I didn't know were arriving, carrying bags and cartons full of food. It looked like the reunion was going to be a big success.

I left the sounds of the celebration behind.

CHAPTER 27

JUNE

Caterina Giovanni

"What do you know about the constellations?" I asked Sam. The bright lights from the city and the wisps of clouds from an earlier rainstorm obscured much of the night sky, but I could still see a few stars suspended above us as we walked through the institute parking lot.

"Uh, they have something to do with horoscopes?" Sam opened his car door for me, and I got in. Sister Beckett had had to stay late to talk with some students, and Sam had offered to give me a ride home.

"Don't you learn how to navigate with the stars in Boy Scouts or something?" I asked him as he climbed in the driver's seat and started the car.

"I didn't," Sam said. "I missed out on that merit badge. What about you? You're in college. Shouldn't you know about that kind of thing?"

"I should, but I don't." As we drove into the night, I glanced out the window at the stars again. I vowed to myself that when I got back to Ithaca, I would find an astronomy book and study the stars. Maybe Steve would want to learn about them with me before he left.

"I know how to use a compass," Sam told me. "And I can tie a bunch of different kinds of knots."

"Impressive. So you're not *completely* without survival skills."

"Not completely." Sam pretended to be offended. "Why? What can *you* do?"

"I know how to build a fire and set up a tent." Sam looked unimpressed, so I added, "And I can catch and fillet a fish with my bare hands."

Sam laughed. "No you can't."

"Well, maybe not that last one," I admitted. "Anyway. So how is everything going with Addie?"

Sam groaned. "You're not going to start up with that again, are you?"

"I can't help it. I like to play matchmaker. Do you know if she's going out with that Rob guy or what?"

"I still haven't asked her about it. What makes you so sure they're not dating?"

"Just a feeling I have. They didn't seem all that into each other on our date last weekend."

"Really?" Sam paused for a second. "I've been thinking about asking her to the graduation dance—"

I didn't let him finish. "Stop thinking about it. Do it. Ask her to the dance."

"What if Rob already asked her?"

"Then ask her out for another night." I sighed. "Seriously, Sam, this doesn't have to be as hard as you're making it."

"What about you?" Sam said. "I heard you have this guy you like back in New York. What are you going to do about that?"

"How did you know about that?" I was stunned.

Sam laughed. "Andrea told her brother, Ethan, and he told Mikey, and Mikey told me."

I blinked. "I guess I shouldn't underestimate the power of the Mormon gossip network around here."

"No you shouldn't," Sam agreed. "I know everything. His name is Steve, and he's going on a mission to Germany and—"

"Andrea is in *so* much trouble," I complained.

"Well? What are you going to do about him when you get home?"

"We can talk about Steve *after* we talk about Addie."

Sam grinned at me. "Then I guess we won't be talking about either one of them."

"Fine."

"Fine."

I opened my mouth to convince Sam to ask Addie to the dance, but then closed it. I remembered how I'd thought I'd known what was going on with Jenna, and how I had guessed wrong time and time again. I hadn't known the whole story with Jenna, and I didn't know it with Addie and Sam either. I decided not to say anything after all. "Never mind. You'll do the right thing. I shouldn't try to boss you around."

Sam tapped his thumbs on the steering wheel. "Thanks. You know, for . . ." He paused.

"For not bossing you around?"

"For being a good friend."

I smiled at him. "You too."

Sam pulled into the Beckett's driveway, and I got out of the car. Sam followed me up the walk.

"This is the last time I'll see you, isn't it?" he asked me.

"I think so. My flight leaves tomorrow morning."

"You have my e-mail and everything, don't you?"

"Yup. And you have mine, right?"

"I do." Sam paused. "Well, if this is the last time I see you, I should give you this." He gave me a giant bear hug, which reminded me of Steve. I hugged Sam back, and then we stepped apart, smiling at each other.

"Keep in touch," I told him, and he nodded. I opened the door, but didn't go inside just yet. Instead, I said to him, "Good luck with the mission and everything."

He smiled. "Thanks. I'll need it."

I think he knew that by "everything," I meant Addie.

• • •

My suitcase was sitting on my bed. There were only a few things left to pack the next morning: my pajamas, my toothbrush, and a plastic "Seattle" snow globe that Chloe had given me as a good-bye present. It wouldn't take long, and then I would be gone.

I turned the snow globe upside down and then back the right way up. The glitter inside showered down over the plastic skyline, over the Space Needle, the Columbia Tower, and the Rainier Tower. There was also a plastic boat glued to the plastic water. If I could have chosen what to put in the snow globe, I would have put the institute building, the waterfront park where I'd gone with Sam and his friends, and the low, glass-fronted building where I'd worked at the research center. That had been *my* Seattle. That and all the people I'd met.

Most of the glitter had fallen and settled at the base of the snow globe, but a few stray pieces still floated, suspended above the miniature skyline. I felt like my time in Seattle had been part of a suspended life, a life I needed to live that was different from my school life or my life in Ithaca.

Maybe I needed to be a little lonely so I could understand how Jenna had felt. Everyone here had been nice to me, and I'd made friends like Sam and Chloe and Sister Beckett. Still, I had felt out of place. Not like the new kid at school, exactly, but like the kid who had moved in a couple of years ago, and who had carved out a spot for herself, but who still didn't know all the history or the nuances of each inside joke.

I opened the window to let the cool night air in, and then I climbed into bed, pulled up my comforter, and thought about Ithaca and Steve. I wondered what it would be like to go back. Suddenly, I couldn't wait to be home.

CHAPTER 28

JUNE

Addie Sherman

Avery came and stood in the doorway of the kitchen, where I was mixing up another attempt at chocolate-chip Jell-O.

"Hey," I said, "I think I figured out what the problem was last time . . ." My voice trailed off as I looked at her. She was wearing different clothes from the last time I'd seen her just a few minutes before, and the expression on her face was focused and serious.

"Addie, my water just broke."

I felt the color drain from my face. "Oh." I don't know much about childbirth, but I do know you can't go back after that point.

"It's okay. I'm only a week away from my due date, which isn't too bad. But we have to get to the hospital."

"Okay," I said. Then I said it again, more confidently, *"Okay."* I knew how to do that, at least. Our long drives had been doubly useful. I knew exactly how to get to the hospital since we'd driven past it so many times.

"My bag is by the door of my bedroom." Avery pulled her hair back into a ponytail and slid on her shoes. "Can you grab it for me and meet me in the car?"

"Of course." I ran up the stairs so fast, I fell flat on my face halfway up, slamming my nose into the hardwood floor. It killed. *Slow down, Addie,* I told myself. I glanced in the hall mirror and saw I had a bloody nose. Wonderful. Just wonderful. There was no time to do anything about it, so I grabbed two tissues and stuck one in each nostril. Then I found Avery's bag and ran back to the car.

"What on earth—?" Avery said from the front seat, staring at the carnage.

"I got so excited I fell down and gave myself a bloody nose." I shoved the suitcase into the backseat and hopped into the front. "It's no big deal."

"The blood is really coming." She sounded queasy. "Are you sure you're okay?"

"I'm sure," I said. I pulled my hoodie off and held it to my face to try to stop the bleeding. "Let's go. Are you ready for this?"

"I'd better be."

While I was driving, Avery called Dave at school. "We're going to the hospital. How fast can you get there?" She listened for a minute. "Addie's with me. I'll see you soon. Love you."

After falling on the stairs in my hurry earlier, I decided I wasn't going to drive even one mile over the speed limit, although every muscle in my body was screaming at me to speed through the inter-sections and get there *now.* They should have a section on this in driver's ed: how to drive carefully and defensively when someone you love is riding in the passenger seat, in labor, and you can't breathe because you're nervous and you have tissues stuffed up your nose.

We got to the hospital safely, and my nose had finally stopped bleeding. A colossal bruise was starting to form across the bridge of my nose and everything was swollen, but at least I could leave the hoodie and the tissues behind.

"Ugh." Avery looked back at the mess I'd made. "It looks like I had the baby in the car."

"Sorry," I told her. She didn't reply. "Avery?"

She was already focused somewhere else. "I'm having a contraction."

By the time we made it to the desk in the hospital lobby, someone had seen enough to get her a wheelchair. We raced through the paperwork and headed up to labor and delivery.

I'd never been in a maternity ward before. I kept my eyes right on Avery, not wanting to look to either side in case I accidentally witnessed someone else's delivery.

"We'll need you to change into this." The nurse placed one of those hospital gowns that look like a giant handkerchief on the papery hospital bedsheet. "Do you need any help?"

"I think I can do it," Avery said.

I turned my back to give her some privacy.

"I'm ready now," she said, and I turned back around. "How do I look?" she asked me. "Completely without dignity, right?"

"You look great." She looked young, and little, but I didn't say that. "Do you want me to leave or stay?"

"Would you mind staying until Dave gets here?"

"Of course not." I pulled a chair over to the bed. "Let me know if you need anything. Otherwise I'll keep my mouth shut."

Avery laughed, and then caught her breath in a contraction. Things were definitely moving along. Where was Dave? I didn't mind hanging out with Avery, or driving her to the hospital, but I really wasn't ready to be in a delivery room.

I was relieved when Dave arrived only a few minutes later, right as the nurse was getting ready to take Avery's blood pressure.

"How are you?" he asked, giving Avery a kiss.

"I'm doing okay so far."

Dave looked over at me. "Thanks for driving, Ad—" He broke off. "Whoa! Did you guys get in a car accident on your way over here?" His eyes flew back to Avery, searching for damage.

"No, I just fell on the stairs." I'd forgotten about my nose.

"Are you all right?"

"I'm fine. Don't worry about me at all."

Dave looked skeptical, but he let the subject drop.

"Is there anything else you guys need me to do before I go?"

Avery shook her head.

"Oh, yeah, there is," Dave said. "Can you call my work and let them know I won't make it in tonight?"

"No problem." Now that Avery was safely at the hospital and in Dave's hands, I was more than ready to be out of there. The nurse announced she needed to check Avery to see how things were progressing. That was my cue.

"Well, I'll get out of your way and go hang out in the waiting room, I think."

"Thanks for everything, Addie," Avery said.

"No problem. Good luck." That seemed to leave too much to chance. "I'll be praying for you guys," I told her. I felt a little self-conscious saying it, but I meant it.

I walked out of the maternity ward the same way I'd walked in: eyes straight ahead, not looking to either side.

I heard someone call, "Excuse me! Excuse me!" but I assumed they were talking to someone else. Then I heard footsteps right behind me. I turned around. It was Avery's nurse, who handed me a slip of paper. "This is for you to take down to the ER to get checked out," she told me. "I think your nose might be broken."

"How long will that take?" I asked. She looked at me in surprise. "I want to be in the waiting room when the baby's born."

"You should be back in time." She smiled. "These things usually take awhile. But you need to get some ice on that nose and get it looked at."

• • •

By the time I came back from the ER, holding an ice pack to my face, the waiting area near the maternity ward was full of people I knew. Avery's parents and sister, Caitlin, were there, and my mom and dad were there too.

"Addie, what happened?" Mom asked in surprise, looking at me. "Where have you been? I was worried!"

"I fell down right before we came to the hospital. My nose is broken. I went down to the ER to get it checked out, and the doctor gave me some ice and some painkillers. There's not much else you can do for a broken nose."

"Oh, Addie." Mom sighed. She has been to the emergency room with my brothers so many times she's kind of passé about injuries.

"Mom, can I borrow your cell phone for a minute? I'm supposed to call Dave's work for him."

She handed me her phone. "Here you go, honey. The number's in there somewhere."

I went around the corner to a quieter part of the waiting area and made the call, shifting the bag of ice on my nose. The cold was blunting the pain and turning things pleasantly numb.

Someone with a very precise voice answered. "Hello, this is Daphne at the Lighthouse."

"Um, hello. This is Addie Sherman. I'm Dave Sherman's sister."

She dropped the carefully modulated tones. "Is his wife having the baby?" she practically squealed.

"Yes, so he won't be in to work for a few days."

"Of course, of course. I'll tell the boss. Is everything going okay?"

"I think so."

"Tell him not to worry about a thing and that we're all thinking of him. This is so exciting!"

It *was* exciting, but we were in for a long wait. My bag of ice turned to water, Avery's little sister got bored, and her dad took her on a walk to see if the gift shop was still open, and my parents both fell asleep, mouths open like fish. Only Avery's mom stayed firmly in position, her purse in her hands, ready to leap to her feet at any moment. Her eyes were fixed anxiously on the hall, and every time a nurse came by she looked hopeful.

Eventually one of the nurses came in. "Mrs. Matthews?" she asked. Avery's mom stood up. "Avery asked me to see if you would like to come in."

"Oh, *yes.*" Avery's mom hurried down the hall without a backward glance. I was glad she was going to be with Avery. Dave's great, but I can't imagine he'd been through childbirth before except when he was born himself.

Not long after Avery's mom left, one of the other waiters from Dave's work brought in dinner for all of us—on the house. It was a surreal dinner, like a scene out of a quirky movie made by independent filmmakers. There we were, hunching over plates on a small scratched plastic end table, sitting on itchy, upholstered chairs, eating Seattle's finest cuisine. The Lighthouse had even sent desserts and drinks, including a bottle of chilled white grape juice in a bucket of ice. "Since Dave doesn't drink champagne, we thought he'd like this," the waiter explained.

"Too bad it's not real champagne," Avery's dad muttered to himself. I could tell he was worried about his daughter. He'd been pacing ever since he and Caitlin had returned from the gift shop.

I knew the cranberry scone with vanilla sauce was Avery's favorite dessert, so I set it aside for her to eat later. Could you eat food right after you'd had a baby? I didn't know, so I asked my mom.

"I think so." She put her arm around me. I didn't pull away. "They'll see what she feels like. I was always starving, but everyone is different."

"I wonder how much longer it's going to be." It was getting late. Avery's mom had been gone for over an hour.

"You never know," Mom said. "This reminds me of when you were born." I stretched out on the couch and rested my head in her lap. She reached out and started stroking my hair, and I let her. I closed my eyes and felt the bandage on my nose, tight and rigid.

"You were born in this very hospital, you know," she said. I knew. "I finally had a daughter—after all those crazy boys."

I knew that, too, but it had been a long time since I'd been willing to listen. She kept talking quietly, and I fell asleep listening to the story of my birth.

. . .

I woke up when Dave came in. He wore hospital scrubs and what looked like a shower cap. His face was tired and illuminated all at once. It had happened.

I sat upright.

"She's here." Dave smiled and tears rolled down his cheeks. "She's little, but she's fine. Healthy and everything. Avery's fine too. She was amazing."

"Oh, wonderful!" my mom said, and my dad said, "Congratulations." I gave Dave a relieved smile.

"You guys can come see her, one at a time," Dave said. "Addie?"

I looked up in surprise. I was first? Dave gestured for me to follow him. I couldn't believe it. I walked with Dave down the hallway. In spite of the usual hospital sounds, it felt almost reverent as we went to Avery's room.

Avery's eyes were closed when I came in, but she wasn't asleep. She opened them the moment she heard our footsteps. In her arms was someone new, a tiny bundle of person with a pink-and-blue-and-white striped cap on top.

"Congratulations," I said softly.

"I wanted you to be one of the first to hold her," Avery said to me. "You did a lot to help get her here safely."

The baby was way too small and way too new for me to hold. She wasn't even two hours old yet. Shouldn't I wait a few days, or weeks? I didn't know if I'd ever held a newborn. But I wanted to hold that little warm compact body so much. I reached out and took her in my arms. The lightness surprised me. "There's nothing to her," I said, and she opened her teeny tiny mouth and let out a squall.

"I take it back." We all laughed, which made her open one dark blue eye and then shut it firmly. She was the result of all of our hard work and love. She was beautiful. I bent over and touched my forehead to hers, careful not to scrape her with the adhesive on my taped-up nose. I blinked back the tears. I'd never been part of a new life like this before.

"So you're naming her after me, right?" I smiled to show them that I was teasing.

"Partly," Avery said. "Adelaide is going to be her middle name."

"Really?" I looked again at the baby and felt flattered that they would name someone so new and so perfect after me. "What's her first name?"

"We're going to combine our names and call her Davery," my brother said.

Avery rolled her eyes at him. "It's Grace," she said. "An old Matthews' family name. My mom's grandmother's name."

"It's beautiful." I looked down at the baby's face again and felt almost a shock of recognition. *So it's you*, I thought. *It's you we've been waiting for and working for, and now, here we are all together, reunited at last.*

Avery started laughing quietly.

"What's so funny?" Dave asked, smiling at her.

"Look at the three of us. Addie with her broken nose, you looking completely exhausted, me with IVs and tubes everywhere. The only one who looks normal is Grace. All this fuss is for her, and she's the only one who made it through unscathed."

"That was the point, right?" I rested my hand on the baby's tiny head one last time before I left the room.

CHAPTER 29

JUNE

Sam Choi

The area around my house is almost all built up. The only groves I know about are on private land or belong to rich people who would have me arrested for trespassing. I could have gone into my backyard to pray, but the hedge between the neighbors' houses was low, and besides, what if they saw me?

Plus, the kind of praying that comes easiest to me is the kind when my eyes are wide open.

It's also easier to pray when Alex isn't around making noise.

So that's how I ended up down by the Kirkland waterfront, looking out over the water and trying to find my courage to start praying. I'd found a spot far out on the pier where Lake Washington was all around me. I could see and hear other people, but I still felt alone and in the middle of something bigger than I was.

There were lots of couples walking along the waterfront, holding hands. Everyone pairs off in the spring. I wondered if Rob and Addie were dating. It didn't seem like they were. They'd been out that one time with me and Cate, but it didn't seem like they were *together*. I might still have a chance. Cate thought I did.

I *should* ask Addie to the graduation dance. I could think of a few ways I might regret that—if Rob got mad at me, or if Addie turned me down, or if we went out and it was awkward and made our friendship weird—but if I didn't ask her, I might regret that even more.

There was too much to think about. I looked out over the water to clear my mind. It was silvery-gray, moving fast or moving slow—but always moving, even in the bay. It lapped against the rocks, against the cement of the retaining wall, against the boats moored at their docks. Always moving.

I sat there for a long time. I didn't have the guts to pray, even though I knew it was time. I'd been reading the scriptures every day since my interview with the bishop. I'd been on splits with the missionaries again, and it had gone better than the last time. I'd fasted the last two Sundays with the purpose of knowing what I should do about a mission. I'd thought about what Ethan and Julie had said. But I still hadn't asked yet. I was wimping out as usual, because I was scared.

What if I didn't get an answer? What if I felt nothing? What if I didn't have a testimony after all?

What if I did?

• • •

Biking home from the waterfront is almost all uphill, so I knew it would take awhile. My parents were probably wondering where I was.

My bike was locked up with a huddle of other bikes. I pulled it out, climbed on, and started riding home.

I went straight through a puddle on purpose. Then another. Then another.

Suddenly I was praying. *What should I do? Are you real? Am I going to be a missionary?* Once I started asking, I couldn't stop. It felt good to reconnect with my faith, like I was coming home from a long trip. I didn't know what I would find when I got there, but I knew it was a place I wanted to be.

I didn't feel an answer yet, but I wasn't disappointed. I knew I was going to keep asking until I got an answer. Until I *knew.* It was time to stop being a wimp. It was time to start living with some conviction, one way or the other. I had to decide. Is this what I believe? Is this who I am?

"Bring it on," I said to myself, as I rode through another puddle. I could do this. I was ready to find out. I would keep reading my scriptures every single day. I would fast every Sunday until I had an answer. The minute I got home, I would call the elders and see if they needed anyone to go on splits with them again next week. I'd keep asking the entire time.

And I was also going to ask Addie to the graduation dance. I owed it to myself to at least try.

"Bring it on," I said again, and I hit another puddle with a satisfying spray. The biggest hill standing between home and me was right ahead, but I had plenty of momentum to get there.

CHAPTER 30

JUNE

Caterina Giovanni

I slid off my flip-flops and let my feet rest in the grass. The ground was warm, and the grass was tickly. I dug my toes in deeper, anchoring myself to the farm and to the summer.

My friend Kayla, whose parents owned the farm, did the same thing. "It's good to have you back, Cate," she told me. "We missed you."

"I missed being here too." It was my first day back on the job as berry supervisor. I loved that almost everything looked the same. The rows of strawberries were bunchy and green, the bright red fruit hanging like heavy Christmas decorations. The little stand next to our lawn chairs where we sat, shaded by the sun, still had the same rusty metal scale and heavy, old cashbox for ringing up customers. Even the customers themselves looked the same—lots of older women picking fruit for canning and making jam, lots of parents with little children, and a few hippies from downtown who loved to support local farmers. Everyone was enjoying the sun and the feeling of being outside in strawberry-smelling air, especially the little kids.

"Have you heard from Steve yet?" Kayla asked.

"Yeah. We're going out tonight." He had called the morning after I'd arrived in Ithaca and invited me on a date. Of course I said yes.

"You'll tell me all about it tomorrow, right?"

Kayla and I had spent most of the morning catching each other up on our lives. We'd told each other the basics in e-mails and phone calls, but now we had a whole summer of sitting side by side to go into detail. It felt wonderful to have time on my hands.

Kayla had forgotten to bring her lunch, so she walked back across the fields to the farmhouse to get it. I waited for her, thinking about some of the questions that had been on my mind since the semester had ended.

I wondered if my roommates and I could truly get to know Jenna next year. What was she really like, when she wasn't fighting addiction and depression and everything else? When she came back in the fall, would we even know her? Had we been any help at all?

I asked myself honestly if I were glad that she was coming back. I decided the answer was yes. I knew we hadn't seen her at her best, but she hadn't seen me at my best either. I'd been judgmental, insecure, and not as nice as I could have been. She was still e-mailing all of us, and I felt like we might all be able to make it through next year now that we knew each other's flaws and strengths better.

I thought about the question that was waiting at the back of my mind for its turn to be asked: What would it be like to see Steve again?

I was distracted by the sound of a car coming up the road. It lurched over the bumps and knots of grass on its way to park near the stand. The car had almost come to a complete stop when I realized *whose* car it was. I stood up suddenly, forgetting to put my flip-flops back on, and took a step forward.

Steve climbed out and looked over at me.

• • •

I think I expected our reunion to be kind of formal. After all, it had been almost a year since we'd last seen each other. I, at least, was feeling nervous and excited and apprehensive. But it's hard to be formal when you're in the middle of a strawberry field and it's summer and you're just so happy to see each other after such a long time.

"It's so good to finally see you," Steve said, reaching out and giving me a huge hug.

"You too." I hugged him back, and neither of us let go for a few seconds.

"I won't stay too long," Steve promised. "I know you're working. But I couldn't wait until tonight. It was driving me crazy knowing you were back in town and I hadn't seen you yet."

"You were the one who went to Florida for Christmas."

"You were the one who went across the country to school."

"You're the one going on a mission," I said, and it was my turn to hug him. "I'm so proud of you."

"You should be. Do you have any idea how freaked out I am about going to Germany?" Then he looked at me. "Actually, you probably do. You're the one who was brave enough to go so far away for school and work."

I liked that. "You want to sit down?" I asked him, gesturing to Kayla's empty lawn chair.

"Will your boss get mad?"

"Not unless you eat the strawberries without paying for them."

Steve sat down in the lawn chair and stretched out his legs. "There are a lot of things I want to tell you."

"Same here," I said. We both grinned at each other.

And then neither of us said anything for a few minutes. Then Steve scooted his lawn chair closer to mine. Then he reached for my hand.

I took a deep breath as I looked out at the landscape of Ithaca. I didn't know if this was always going to be home. I didn't know how everything was going to play out, or who I would end up with, or where I would eventually call home.

Still, it was good to know that I had roots, strong ones, in ground like this.

JUNE

Addie Sherman

Everything was coming up Addie, and I didn't know what to do about it.

Baby Grace was home from the hospital and doing well. The last English test of the year was over, and thanks to Avery and her tutoring, I had passed with a solid B. My parents and I were getting along. I was finally going to my first high school dance.

Avery put the finishing touches on my hair. "This doesn't look very traditional," she warned me.

"Good." I'd wanted my hair to look like Avery's had the day she and Dave got married. She'd worn it long and wavy and loose and had pinned a few flowers in it. I didn't think I was in the market for a hairstyle that required me to have a lot of hair piled up on top of my head. Lots of girls look wonderful like that. Not me. I was sure I'd get a headache or make a mess of it somehow halfway through the night.

"Okay, you can look now. I'm finished." Avery let me turn to face the mirror. "You're beautiful."

Is it bad that I agreed? I'd worried more than I wanted to about the dress, hair, and shoes—the dressing-up-Addie part of this date.

It was both a relief and a surprise to discover that I looked pretty. Maybe not as head-turning as tiny, blonde Brook, or as striking as Avery when she dressed up to go out, but that was fine.

I wasn't Brook or Avery. I was Addie Sherman, and I looked great.

• • •

We still had some time to kill before my date showed up, so Avery and I wandered out into the living room to wait. My mom was holding Grace and turned to look at us the moment she heard our footsteps on the hardwood. "Oh, Addie," Mom said. "You look wonderful."

"Thanks, Mom."

I hoped she would leave it at that, but she couldn't. She had waited a long time to see her only daughter all dressed up for a dance. "Can I take a couple of pictures of you? I won't embarrass you later, I promise. But can I take a few now?"

"All right. I want Avery in the picture too. And then one with you."

We took about five pictures, which for me is basically a photo shoot. "Okay, that's enough," I said, reaching for Grace. Mom handed her to me, but she looked worried.

"What if she spits up on your dress?"

"I don't mind." Just in case, though, I arranged a burp cloth over my shoulder where Grace's head rested.

"So, tell me about the Reonion," I said to Avery, and she laughed. I'd been meaning to talk to her since the big event, but Grace's arrival and the excitement of going to the dance had pushed it out of my mind.

"It went great. Tyler Cruz, this guy from high school, came all the way from Utah for Julie's homecoming. Mikey and Ethan were there, of course, and a bunch of our other friends. Andrea and her husband too. Julie couldn't believe how many people were there. It was perfect."

"I know I've seen Julie before, but I can't remember what she looks like."

"Wait. Here's a picture of her." Avery pulled one of Dave's old yearbooks from the shelf and turned the pages until she found Julie's picture. We both looked at the shyly smiling girl for a minute.

"And here's me." Avery flipped to her picture, and there she was, glaring at the camera. I stared closely at the picture, looking for the Avery I knew now in the high school junior she'd been a few years ago. I could definitely see her in there.

"I'm boring you, right?" Avery said, making a face and starting to close the yearbook.

"No, tell me more. Show me some of the other people." I shifted Grace on my shoulder, and she made a sound somewhere between a hiccup and a squeak. I could feel her breath, so light and soft you might think you'd imagined it, a little sigh from your past or your future. I felt more connected with my family than I had in a long time, and I owed most of that to Avery and Grace.

Avery turned through the pages, pointing out her friends. I could see writing on some of the pages. I wondered what I would think when I looked back on my yearbook and saw Sam, or Rob, or Cody. What would I remember about them, and what would they remember about me?

One thing was for sure. Right now I had friends, good ones.

It seems like everyone is always talking about the love of your life. What about the *friends* of your life? You can have more than one, and at certain times in your life, you need them just as much as the love of your life. Maybe more.

Grace let out an enormous burp, simultaneously filling her pants.

"She gets that from Dave," I told Avery.

• • •

He rang the doorbell right on time, and I went to answer it. I gave Mom and Avery a look that said, "Stay here." I didn't want to go marching out there like a queen with her attendants or a pop star with an entourage. I wanted this to be as low-key as possible so I didn't start feeling awkward and self-conscious.

When I opened the door, the first thing he said was, "Wow."

I felt awkward and self-conscious. "Thanks."

"You look awesome."

"You too."

He reached out to take my arm and noticed I was holding a purse in my hand. "What's in there?" he asked.

"Oh, you know. Lip gloss. Minty gum. Some jerky. We can share it with Cody and his date when we get to the dance."

That made him laugh. "Are you kidding me?"

"No," I said. I opened up the purse to prove it. "See?"

"I should have asked you to a dance a long time ago."

"Because I bring great refreshments?"

"No, seriously. I'm lucky you agreed to go with me to this one."

"Of course I said yes. You're one of my best friends."

"I don't want to take you to this dance as a friend." He reached out and took my hand as we walked to the car. Avery and my mom and Grace were probably watching from the window. I didn't care.

"Oh." I started to smile. "Okay. So we're *not* friends?"

"Oh, we're friends. We're *definitely* friends. You're one of the best friends I've ever had."

I liked the way he said that, like he meant it, and also like he meant something more too.

He opened the car door for me, but I didn't get in, and he didn't step away from the door. We stood there, looking at each other.

"Is your mom watching from the window?" he asked.

I snuck a peek over his shoulder. "Not that I can see."

"Good." He moved closer, and I knew what was about to happen, and I couldn't wait, so I moved closer too.

It was a night of firsts: first dance, first kiss, and, the photographer told us, the first time he'd taken a picture at a formal dance where the guy was wearing a star-spangled ski hat.

REUNION

Before the sealing, he entered the temple alone. After, he left the temple alone. No pictures, no family members, no flowers or congratulations. He wore a suit, not a tuxedo. He wore her favorite tie, now slightly out of style. His hair, which was almost entirely gray, was freshly trimmed and neatly combed. He was not a young man, the way he had been on his first wedding day, but he had still taken care of his appearance.

He walked with buoyancy in his step, floating on hope, until he reached his car. Then, he wept a little as he drove home. The pain was familiar, and he acknowledged it, but the hope was new. The hope helped him move past the pain more quickly than he had in the past. Now, there was a chance. Now, he might be with her forever.

Mr. Thomas walked into the front room of his home and picked up the picture of himself and his wife. "Happy anniversary," he said. Even with his new faith, he wasn't positive about how these things worked.

He wasn't completely sure if she could hear him.

He thought she could.

ACKNOWLEDGMENTS

First and foremost, I want to thank the fans of the Yearbook series. It has been way too much fun to write these books and to hear back from you regarding the characters and their stories. I hope you enjoy this last (for now, anyway) book in the series. I am so grateful for your support, and I thought of you as I wrote every page. This book is for you.

I also want to express my gratitude to:

My line-of-first-defense readers, Bob and Elaine, who exhibit the perfect combination of brutal honesty and unfailing help.

My round-two readers: Nic, Hope, Arlene, Libby Parr, Jana Hay, Kirk Bulloch, and Joree Hansen. Thank you for the time and effort you invested in helping me with *Reunion*.

The wonderful professionals at Deseret Book: Lisa Mangum, Chris Schoebinger, Tonya Facemyer, and Ken Wzorek.

My little boys, who help me keep my priorities straight. Writing can always wait, but a full juice cup, a clean diaper, and/or a ride to preschool can't.

Acknowledgments

My husband, who is a part of it all, from listening to the beginnings of a new idea to reading the final draft.

Finally, I have realized that I have been blessed with unusually wonderful friends throughout my life. Although *Reunion* is a story about love, it is also a story about friendship. I am deeply grateful for the friends over the years who have known me at various stages of awkwardness and ineptitude (high school, college, newly-married, young mother), and who have loved and supported me anyway.

ABOUT THE AUTHOR

Allyson Braithwaite Condie received a degree in English teaching from Brigham Young University. She went on to teach high school English in Utah and in upstate New York for several years. She loved her job because it combined two of her favorite things—working with students and reading great books.

Currently, however, she is employed by her three little boys, who keep her busy playing trucks and building blocks. They also like to help her type and are very good at drawing on manuscripts with red crayon. She enjoys running with her husband, reading, traveling, and eating.